THEY WALK AMONG US

A COLLECTION OF UTAH HORROR

Other books by The Utah Horror Writers

Old Scratch and Owl Hoots: A Collection of Utah Horror

It Came from the Great Salt Lake: A Collection of Utah Horror

Apocalypse Utah: A Collection of Utah Horror

The Hunger: A Collection of Utah Horror

Peaks of Madness: A Collection of Utah Horror

Other books by Forty—Two Books

Putrescent Poems: Horror Poetry Vol 1

Satan Speaks! Contemporary Satanic Voices

Monster Brain: Conversations with OCD

Strange Stories Volume 1

The Dress: A Poetic Response

All titles are available on Amazon

THEY WALK AMONG US

A COLLECTION OF UTAH HORROR

An anthology of original Utah horror by the Utah Horror Writers

April 2020

Edited by Daniel Cureton
and Joni B. Haws

42
Books

Salt Lake City

Forty-Two Books, LLC.
Salt Lake City, UT, USA.
www.fortytwobooks.com
Cover art by Carter Reid, www.thezombienation.com
Printed in USA on acid free paper. Times New Roman, Underworld, and Requiem fonts

ISBN-13: 978-1-7340067-6-6
Library of Congress Control Number: 2019920546

Editors

Daniel Cureton, MA
www.danielcureton.com
Joni B. Haws

LETTER FROM THE EDITORS

In this 6th installment of the anthology you will find original content by authors from the state of Utah and beyond. Each has taken the time to submit, be judged under blind peer-review, and work with editors to polish their craft up to standard for publication.

Enjoy the scares,

Daniel Cureton,
Joni B. Haws
January 12, 2020
Salt Lake City, UT, USA

Bestiary List

Letter from the Editors v

Bestiary List vi

Part .V: Catechism

Introduction ix

Part .III/VTH: Venatores

Biographies xi

Part I: Jaunts

Flash Fiction

The Hellveteen Rabbit 19

Julie Frost

The Babysitter 24

E. Ellis Allen

In Wolf's Clothing 29

Cass Carvajal

Dinner for Halgaroth 32

Heidi Voss

Part II: Balladry

Poetry

Werewolf Approaches His nineties 37

John Grey

Companionship 38

Scott Darrington

THE TRICK IS TO LET THEM THINK WHAT THEY WANT TO THINK 40

Juleigh Howard-Hobson

TREASURE 42

David C. Kopasak-Merkel

MIRRORS NEVER LIE 44

C.H. Lindsay

ANGUISH 45

Steven F. Craner

THE WEREDOODLE OF WASATCH HOLLOW 48

Alan J. MacFarlane

ROTTEN MOONSHINE 56

C.H. Lindsay

PART III: EXPEDITIONS

NOVELETTES

GOOD FENCES 59

Julie Frost

THE DEEP TIMBER 100

C.R. Langille

PART IV: QUESTS

SHORT FICTION

NO SOLICITING 139

Caryn Larrinaga

THE WILD HUNT 157

Cecily Kingston

HER SKIN 163

Maegan Langer

RESISTER 178

Lehua Parker

NIGHT WATCH 201

Madeline M. Marcum

Part .V: Catechism

Introduction from the Publisher

The Utah Horror Writers is creating a great legacy of content and writing in the state of Utah. The act of producing and pushing content to the public eye shows the vibrant and diverse culture that exists in Deseret. A healthy society embraces and encourages its hidden components (as horror often is).

Regardless of its historical origins and political affiliations, a culture that expresses itself in the many ways in which peoples exist and live is a culture that flexes with change and reinvests in itself for the future. Horror is often one of the elements of culture that is suppressed and banned by the dominate structures in a society (governments, officials, churches) because of the inherent nature of what it contains: upsetting, disturbing, moral defying, and challenging ideas which can transform an individual.

From the things that go bump in the night, to gore, repulsion, fright, terror, and what makes us uncomfortable, horror at its core is not about shock value or exposition. Though exposition, grindhouse, and body horror have their place, the use of horror in human culture dates back to ancient times with folk myths and fairy tales—scaring children into behaving—warning of danger, and exciting the minds to the possibilities of adventure.

Horror can act as a medium to express imagination, ethical lessons, and to understand what it means to be human by reflecting on a situation which isn't real, but very well could be. The genre and the creativity within invites discussion, confronts assumptions, and makes us turn inward to answer the questions about how we feel and how we will live our lives after encountering the most terrifying and horrific monsters of all: ourselves.

Each story is a piece of art, put together in a collection that is a public exhibition. Creative writing, as a fine art, allows us to tame the inner demons and befriend the outer monsters of the world.

It is my aim as a publisher to produce fine craft and writing that is of high caliber—showing talent—old and new. In this installment, Forty-Two Books is pleased to present the best and most original horror of Utah:

THEY WALK AMONG US

In Screams,
Daniel Cureton, MA
Salt Lake City, UT
January 23, 2020

PART .III/V^TH: VENATORES

Author Biographies

Alan J. Macfarlane has Utah roots that run deep, descending from Brigham Young and other Mormon pioneer stock. A graduate from the University of Utah, Alan has spent more than a decade as a writer, editor, and creative director in Utah's "Silicon Slopes" tech scene. He thanks his wife, Anna, for accompanying him to too many scary movies and humoring his love of the macabre. His four kids are also infected with a love of ghost stories and Halloween, for which Alan is very proud. And lastly, he thanks Freddie, his mini goldendoodle for inspiring Alan's entry to this collection.

Cecily Kingston is a writer, artist, and musician. She loves the horror genre, but has never written any horror stories before this. She is extremely excited to be a part of this anthology. Cecily plays eight instruments and enjoys hiking and kickboxing in her free time.

C. H. Lindsay is an award-winning writer & poet, housewife, and mother—not necessarily in that order. She spent thirty years as an event planner, helping organize and run science fiction, fantasy, and horror conventions, and a decade acting in musicals. Now she prefers to stay at home with her family and write novels, short stories, and poetry. This is her ninth anthology. She's a member of SFWA, HWA, SFPA, and LUW. Mostly blind, she lives in Utah with her "seeing-eye husband," son, and a cat who thinks she's another child.

C.R. Langille spent many a Saturday afternoon watching monster movies with his mother. It wasn't long before he started crafting nightmares to share with his readers. An avid hunter and outdoorsman, C.R. Langille incorporates the Utah wilderness in many of his tales. He is an affiliate member of the Horror Writer's Association, a member of the League of Utah Writers, and received his MFA: Writing Popular Fiction from Seton Hill University.

Cass Carvajal writes horror and dark fantasy stories, often inspired by folklore. By day she works as an accountant in Salt Lake City, where she lives with her husband and dog.

Caryn Larrinaga is a horror evangelist and paranormal junkie from Salt Lake City, Utah. She loves animals, chai tea, and spookiness, and she tries to write those things into her award-winning fiction as much as possible. Watching scary movies through split fingers terrified Caryn as a child, and those nightmares inspire her to write now. Find her supernatural cozy mystery novels, *The Soul Searchers Mysteries*, wherever books are sold, and visit www.carynlarrinaga.com for free short stories and audiobooks.

David C. Kopaska-Merkel assumed human form in the 50's. As a cover, he edited *Star*line* in the late '90s, and won the Rhysling award (long poem) in 2006 for "The Tin Men" (a collaboration with Kendall Evans). His poetry has been published in venues including Asimov's, Strange Horizons, Polu Texni, Primate Cuisine, & Night Cry. He has written 31 books and edits *Dreams and Nightmares magazine; @DavidKM on Twitter.*

E. Ellis Allen When not writing her daydreams into stories, E. Ellis Allen is catching up on True Crime Podcasts, and strategizing on how to get ice cream on the bottom of the food pyramid, and how to practice knife throwing in four-inch heels. E. is a wife and mother of two young adults and a canine custodian of a bilingual Chiweenie on the Spectrum. She has been featured in several Anthologies and writes a blog featuring a mix of book reviews called Book Bites, as well as perspectives on the joys and tragedies of life. Visit her @ girlonstilts.com, and Facebook.com/eellisallen.

Heidi Voss is terrified of terraforming her Animal Crossing island for fear of messing it up, and has been drawing for the first time in years because her MMA gym has been closed. You can check out her self-isolation collages on Twitter @rarevoss, or visit her website at authorheidivoss.com for more short stories and, eventually, a release date for her forthcoming novel *Frogman's Response.*

John Grey is an Australian poet, US resident. Recently published in *Sin Fronteras*, *Dalhousie Review,* and *Qwerty* with work upcoming in *Plainsongs*, *Willard* and *Connecticut River Review*.

Julie Frost is an award-winning author who writes every shade of speculative fiction. Her short stories appear in

Straight Outta Dodge City, *Monster Hunter Files*, *Writers of the Future*, *Tales of Ruma*, and many others. Her werewolf series, Pack Dynamics, is published by WordFire Press, and her novel *Dark Day, Bright Hour* is published by Ring of Fire Press. She whines about writing, a lot, at http://agilebrit.livejournal.com/

Juleigh Howard-Hobson's poetry has appeared in scores of journals across the world, including *Polu Texni*, *Coffin Bell*, *Eye to the Telescope*, *Noir Nation*, *The Literary Hatchet,* and others. Her fifth poetry collection is the Elgin nominated *Our Otherworld* (Red Salon Press). She lives in the cold grey Pacific Northwest where she writes numinous poetry and avoids the woods at night. She has been nominated for several prizes including The Pushcart, Best of the Net, Rhysling, and Elgin. Find her on Twitter: ForestPoet@PoetForest.

Lehua Parker writes speculative fiction stories for kids and adults that are often set in her native Hawaii. Her published works include the Niuhi Shark Saga trilogy, Lauele Chicken Skin Stories, and Lauele Fractured Folktales, as well as various plays, poetry, short stories, and essays. An advocate of indigenous voices, she is a frequent speaker at conferences, schools, and symposiums.

Madeline M. Marcum's fiction has previously appeared in *Metaphor*. In 2019, her short story "Monsters in the Woods" was accepted for presentation at the National Undergraduate Literary Conference. She graduated from Weber State University with her dream degree in creative writing and literary editing. Madeline enjoys dabbling with the new and unexpected in a wide variety of story lengths and genres, as well as spending time in the writing community throughout the year. She lives in Herriman, UT with her amazingly supportive husband and more notebooks than she will ever use. Read about Madeline's latest projects and ventures at madelinemmarcum.com.

Maegan Langer has been a horror fan since she was seven years old, when her mom let her stay up late one night to watch *Alien* on TV. She earned a biology degree from Brigham Young University, but snuck in creative writing classes to stay sane. Her personal essay, "Alternative Goddess" appeared in the March/April 2008 issue of *Cicada* magazine and her short story, "Alpine Slide" was published in the Utah Horror Writers 2019 anthology, *The Peaks of Madness.*

Scott Darrington is a poet in Provo, Utah, who edits dental websites by day and goes to sleep at a reasonable hour at night. His favorite writers are George Herbert, Robert Francis, and Steven Erikson. His favorite horror film is *Alien.* He is currently working on a poetry-prose project about a man who talks with ghosts and tries to avoid losing his mind.

Steven F. Craner has lived in Utah his entire life, with a brief stint in the Coast Guard. Married for over 43 years, he has 5 children, 4 grandsons, but no pets at the present time. Steve enjoys gardening, yoga, walking, inside and outside Bonsai, playing Blues and Roots music, reading, writing poetry, and spending time traveling in Utah, Idaho and Montana with his beautiful wife Catherine. He started writing poetry in the fifth grade after the encouragement of a wonderful teacher, then forgot all about writing for several decades. About ten years ago he began writing poetry again with a renewed vigor as a way of pursuing some much needed personal exploration and rediscovery.

Part I: Jaunts

ΔΦ ff

Flash Fiction

The Hellveteen Rabbit

Julie Frost

"I hate the new baby," Elsie confided to Herbie, her plush bunny. They snuggled under the covers together. She'd been awakened by her little brother's crying again, and now she couldn't get back to sleep.

She used one hand to turn Herbie's head toward her and the other to wiggle his ears. She'd had him ever since she could remember, along with a copy of *The Velveteen Rabbit*. Elsie had latched onto the story, and she was positive that Herbie was real. Most of his fur had rubbed off, especially around his neck, and his nose had disappeared. His eyes were made of glass, and one had been crunched against the side of the dryer, giving him a rather crazed aspect that only made her adore him more.

"I don't like him either," Elsie made Herbie say in special bunny-speak. "But I love you, Elsie."

"I love you too, Herbie." She yawned, hugged him, and fell asleep.

Δ

“Elsie!” Mommy called. “Did you put Herbie in Kevin’s crib?”

Elsie’s eyes popped open. Herbie wasn’t with her? No, he wasn’t. Mommy stood in the doorway, one hand on her hip, dangling him by the ears with the other. He hated that. “What have we told you about things in the crib? Kevin’s too little for that right now, sweetie, and it’s not safe for Herbie to be there when he’s sleeping. When he’s older you can share.”

Like she’d want to share Herbie with a stinky baby. Why did they have to have a baby, anyway?

“I didn’t,” Elsie said. “Maybe he hopped there by himself.”

Mommy gave her that Look and tossed Herbie onto the bed. “Uh-huh. Come downstairs and have breakfast.”

Eating her cornflakes, Elsie puzzled over what was so special about Kevin. All he did was eat, poop, and cry, and he needed lots of attention for no apparent reason. Herbie sat on the table beside her, and he was confused, too.

After breakfast, Elsie went to kindergarten, leaving Herbie to stand guard over her toys. As soon as she came home, she went to get him, but he was gone. “Mommy? Where’s Herbie?”

“Not my job to keep track of your stuff, honey.” Mommy seemed tired. She was tired a lot, lately. “Where’d you leave him?”

“Right *here*.”

“Are you sure?”

Not answering, she poked through her downstairs toy-box, but he wasn't there. He wasn't in her room either. She peeked into the baby's room.

Herbie crouched in the crib by Kevin's head. "Naughty bunny," Elsie whispered, not wanting to awaken the Scream Machine. She tiptoed over, grabbed the rabbit, and ran back to her room.

"Why do you keep going in the baby's room?" she asked. "Do you like that stinky baby more than me now?"

"No!" Herbie's bunny-speak was indignant. "I don't like the baby at all."

"Maybe..." Elsie's voice dropped to a whisper. "Maybe we should get rid of him. Then Mommy wouldn't be so tired all the time, and she'd pay more attention to us."

"Mm-hm." Elsie nodded Herbie's head.

Elsie had no idea how to accomplish such a thing. But Herbie was smart. He'd figure it out.

±A±

The next morning, Mommy stood in Elsie's doorway again, holding Herbie by his ears and frowning. "Elsie! What did I tell you about putting your bunny in Kevin's crib?"

"I didn't!"

"Don't lie to me. How else would he get there?"

"I don't know. But I didn't put him there!"

Mommy had that Look again, and Elsie was scared. She hadn't put Herbie in the crib, but Mommy didn't believe her. "Keep better track of your things." She dropped Herbie onto the floor and left.

Elsie spanked Herbie. “Bad bunny. You’re getting us in trouble.”

±A±

“This is the third time this stupid rabbit’s been in Kevin’s crib in the morning!” Mommy shook Herbie while Elsie cried. “That’s it! You’ll get him back in a week!”

“But I didn’t!” Elsie’s pleas were in vain, and Herbie sat way up high in the closet. With his ears flattened and his crushed eye glaring, he looked angry.

When she came home from kindergarten, Mommy sent her for a nap, snapping “No!” when Elsie asked if she could sleep with Herbie. Elsie trudged upstairs and lay down, arms crossed over her chest. “It’s all the baby’s fault,” she muttered. “I wish he’d just die.” She wasn’t going to sleep. No, she wasn’t.

But she did.

She woke to find Herbie sitting on her chest. Surprised, she grabbed him, kissed his nose, and buried her face in his belly fur. “Did Mommy forgive you?”

At least, that’s what she tried to say.

Herbie had fastened himself over her face. At first it was funny, and she giggled. Herbie was hugging her back! But when she tried to inhale, the fun abruptly stopped. He wouldn’t move. “You awakened me, but you can’t make me real,” he growled.

Elsie wanted to ask why, because surely she loved him

enough, but her mouth was full of fur and her mind was full of fear. He answered anyway. "You have to love your whole family, not just me. Nursery magic is funny that way."

She couldn't get him off. "You've said over and over how much you hate Kevin." Couldn't see. "Today you wanted him to die." Couldn't speak. "You're curdled inside, Elsie. I can't be real if I'm yours." Couldn't breathe. "And, for the record? I like Kevin just fine."

Couldn't scream.

She scrabbled, yanking on any part of him she could in her panic. Ears, feet, fur—nothing made a difference. Her struggles weakened, and her hands...weren't...working...

An hour later, her mother screamed enough for both of them, but it was too late.

Herbie sat on the shelf, giving nothing away.

±A±

The week after the funeral, Elsie's parents moved the stuffed bunny into the baby's room, as a memento of the sister he'd never know.

Herbie watched everything from his new perch in Kevin's bookcase. Waiting, again, to become Real.

The Babysitter

E. ELLIS ALLEN

As soon as my mommy and daddy back out of the driveway, Anna tells me to lock the door with the deadbolt and chain.

"What about Maggie?" I ask.

"I'm the babysitter tonight," Anna says.

The others gather the candles and matches. Anna says she has a new game for us and keeps it in a white bag. We follow her up the stairs.

Once in the attic, Anna pulls up the trapdoor and draws the curtain over the window. It's freezing up here, and our breath turns into clouds, and my fingers burn with ice. It's cold and dark when we play our games.

Anna directs us to our spots in the center of the room. We settle in a row, oldest to youngest.

"I want to be the leader!" Edith complains. "I've been in the woods the longest!"

"Shut up!" Anna tells her. "I'm the leader because I'm the oldest. Besides, I know how to play this game!"

"What's the game?" Edith wants to know.

"It's special," Anna says. "I found it just for her."

"Me?" I ask.

"Yes, it's an initiation."

Edith grins.

"It's what?" I ask.

"You want to be one of us, don't you?" Anna tips her head and waits for me to nod.

Taylor is crying. She cries a lot. I light the candles, and she calms down. Edith is never scared and never cries. I think it's because she's from the woods and is used to the dark. I don't think Anna knows how to be scared.

Anna is smiling and places the bag on her lap, and Taylor starts to cry all over again.

"Shut up, Taylor," Anna yells. "You're such a baby! Shut up, or I'll blow out the candles!"

Taylor sticks her thumb in her mouth, and I pat her head.

"How do you know how to play?" Edith asks.

"I read it in a book," Anna says and shows her a book.

Edith grins.

The game begins the same way all the others do with Anna dragging the piece of white chalk behind us, drawing a circle. But this time she is drawing something else in the middle.

"What's that?" I ask.

"It's going to be a star," Edith says.

"No! Don't! Stop!"

"Shut up, Taylor!" Anna says. She tells us to sing the song, so we do.

"The more we are together, together, together, the more we are together, the happier we'll be!"

When Anna is finished drawing, she sits in the middle of the star and holds the white bag. She tells us to close our eyes and hold out our hands. We do.

She takes from the bag a small heavy thing and passes it. We each touch the cold metal. We hold it and feel its curves and smooth handle, and the round opening of its nose.

Anna takes it back and then tells us to hold out our hands again and to keep our eyes closed. We do.

I feel something drop in my hands. It's small and tube-shaped with a flat bottom on one end and a rounded tip on the other. It smells like the fireplace. Ann takes it back.

"Keep your eyes closed," Anna tells us. We do.

I hear a click and then feel the heavy thing in my hand, again.

"Here, you have to hold it like this, now," Anna says and helps me. "Steady…steady…"

I feel cold metal press against my forehead.

Taylor is crying harder.

"Shut up!" Anna says. "Keep your eyes closed, it'll only be a second!"

I hear the wind. It seeps through the roof and the cracks in the walls. It whistles and whistles, and seems to make the light bulb grow brighter and brighter.

"Hurry," Edith cries.

"Shut up!"

The wind howls and howls, it shrieks until my ears

hurt and until the light bulb breaks, and the candles blow out. Everybody screams.

The wind stops howling. The heavy thing is taken out of my hands. We wait in the dark for something to happen. I blink, but I can't see any of them in the blackness. I blink but then can't open my eyes.

Far away, I hear banging. The banging gets louder until it seems I'm sitting on top of each knock. I hear my parents calling my name.

I hear the creak of the trapdoor opening and hear the ladder spilling out. I still can't open my eyes.

My daddy carries me downstairs to the couch. My mommy rubs warmth back into my arms, legs, and face until I open my eyes.

"For crying out loud!" Daddy yells. "What is going on around here?"

"Honey?" Mommy says, "What happened? Did you forget your babysitter was coming over? You dead-bolted the door, and she couldn't get in."

Maggie, the teenager from next door, is sitting on the chair by the fireplace. She wrinkles her nose at me.

"And what about these?" Daddy yells. He points to the candles. "And where on earth did you find this?" He showed me the gun.

Mommy gasps.

"Where's Anna?" I say. "Where are Edith and Taylor? We can't leave them up there, Taylor's afraid of the dark!"

"What are you talking about?" Daddy yells. "Who's

that? Are they the idiots who brought the gun?"

"Honey, have you met some friends already?" Mommy asks. She holds my hands. Her hands are much warmer than mine. I can see the whites of her eyes all the way around.

I tell them who my new friends are. I say Anna lived in my room once, but now she lives in the attic, and Edith is from the woods. And I tell them Taylor's the missing girl buried beneath the swimming pool next door.

"Who?" Maggie asks. She stands up and her eyes are wide. "Did you say, Taylor?"

Then Maggie begins to scream.

In Wolf's Clothing

CASS CARVAJAL

When Abigail finished vomiting up the flesh of the campers, she shrugged the wolfskin the rest of the way off and tossed it into the fire. Simon did not at first think that it would burn. Any heavy fur should have smothered the weak fire left in the pit, and this was no ordinary fur.

But the flames caught, and quickly. Tongues of flame consumed the coat with unnatural speed, and dark, foul-smelling smoke drifted up towards the dark sky.

Abigail watched it burn, hellfire reflecting in her eyes. She trembled now, though from horror or cold Simon wasn't sure. Without her coat, she was clad in nothing but blood and tears.

The tears were her own. The blood was not.

"Now yours." Abigail nodded to Simon's own coat and jerked her head toward the fire. "Burn it."

Simon looked down at the blood-matted fur in his hands. He stroked it thoughtfully.

It started as a joke.

They'd gone to a thrift shop in search of cheap Halloween costumes. Simon had almost overlooked the hideous things in the bargain bin, digging through heaps of stale-smelling polyester and stained sequin dresses. But then his fingers had met soft, warm fur, and he'd pulled out the skins.

They were huge, with thick, grey-brown fur on one side and smooth hide on the other. Real fur, not that fake plastic stuff, and all seemingly in one piece. Simon couldn't guess what animal they'd come from.

He couldn't say now why he showed the skins to Abigail. At the time, he'd just thought that his find was hilarious. He expected Abigail to pull a face and tell him to put the roadkill back where he'd found it. He'd sauntered over to her, one skin half-draped over his shoulders, one held out toward her, waggling his eyebrows suggestively.

"What do you think?"

Abigail had barked a laugh.

"Those are the ugliest things I've ever seen!" She'd declared it with delight. "We're buying them."

And they did. The coats were a dollar each. A steal, Abigail had called it. "We'll be the tackiest werewolves in history."

It wasn't until they got home that they finally tried the skins on. Abigail wrapped hers around herself like a shawl, strutting around the bedroom with her head held high like some sort of mangy Old Hollywood starlet. Simon draped his own fur around his shoulders and over his head, a thrift-store

Hercules. The laughed and posed and took pictures, and then, when the novelty wore off, they tried to take the skins off.

Tried. The skins would not come off.

Things got a little fuzzy after that. Simon remembered running. He remembered the smell of pine and fallen leaves, of cold mountain air. He remembered the hot copper of blood, warm and sweet as hot cider on his tongue. For days they had wandered, wild-eyed and feral. For days they had killed whoever had crossed their path. Until tonight, when at last the skins had come loose and slipped from their shoulders.

The still-hot liver had slipped from Simon's hands and hit the dirt with a wet thump. Abigail had wailed, tossing the half-eaten heart away and stumbling away from the carnage to vomit.

"Burn it!" Abigail said again.

It was his first thought, too, when he woke from the blood-frenzy and the horror of what they'd done began to sink in. He'd killed people. He'd eaten people. Even now the blood of the campers coated his lips, organ flesh stuck between his teeth. He'd never be able to eat meat again without remembering the taste of biting into human flesh.

Burn the skin, and it would never happen again. Could never happen again.

Simon licked his lips.

He donned the skin once more.

Dinner for Halgaroth

Heidi Voss

In the many lonely nights I've pictured myself being tied up by a beautiful woman, this is not what I was after.

"Can we talk about this?"

"Halgaroth needs a monthly sacrifice. It's nothing personal." She draws a chalk circle on the concrete floor of her sorority's basement. This is so dumb. I don't even go to this school. My buddy Mike was so set on getting laid at a sorority party.

"Is this why you're all so pretty?" I should have higher priority questions, but I'm still very much buzzed.

"No, that's just contouring. If I wasn't going to sacrifice you to a demon of infinite wisdom, I'd send you a YouTube tutorial."

I wish I could come up with a great reason for her to keep me alive, but I'm struggling. "It's wrong" seems too obvious. "I'm a nice guy" would be a lie.

"Oh my god, is that a Steak and Shake gift card?" She thumbs through the cards in my wallet. "I used to love going there after football games." She has stopped lighting ceremonial candles.

"Yeah, you from Ohio too?"

"Troy."

"The strawberry festival?"

"Oh my god!" She holds her cheeks in her hands. "My mom still sends me pictures of the strawberry pies. The seafood festivals out here in Baltimore are not the same."

I take a shot in the dark. She's tall.

"Volleyball player?"

"Softball. I wasn't good enough to get a scholarship, but Halgaroth helps with that." She strikes a match and lights the last candle in the circle.

The earth shakes as cracks forms in the cement of the chalk circle. Clawed, blue hands emerge from below, digging into the basement floor. A smell like putrid scabs and ripe peaches fills the room.

The creature that pulls itself forth has a head like a lion, but the mouth is too big. Its hot breath hits my face and I choke on the stench. They're about to wrap their too many teeth around my head when the woman says,

"Hey, Hal, he's from Troy, too."

Halgaroth draws back, eyes shining.

"Used to go to the strawberry festival."

They set their head on a leathery hand. "Hast thou a crush on the sacrifice?"

The woman's cheeks go pink. "Hal, he's right here."

Halgaroth puts a hand to their chest. "I believed thy attention wast mine alone." They gesture to the candles, the chalk circle. "Is this a ruse? Art thou using me for my tuition funds alone?"

"It's not like that!" She holds up her hands, backing away. "I miss those strawberry pies."

Halgaroth turns their six eyes to me. My hands shake.

"I require sacrifice. Shall I consume you, or her?"

My eyes go from Halgaroth, to the girl, and back. I know what the noble, right answer is, but like I said, I'm not a nice guy.

Part II: Balladry

ΔΦЋ

Poetry

Werewolf Approaches His Nineties

John Grey

The moon's not what it was.
It barely nudges the hairs in my palms.
And my chin and cheeks are frustratingly smooth.
I still have the hunger, but it's deep inside me,
a pitiable combination of incessant memory
and arthritic desire. I can barely rise from this chair.
My fingernails stubbornly refuse to grow.
And what about my teeth—
Missing, mostly, and the few survivors
are blunt as my fresh-from-college doctor
when we discuss the state of my health.
Nightly, I hear the wolves
howl from deep in the woods.
Rub it in, why don't you.

COMPANIONSHIP

SCOTT DARRINGTON

"Oh, that's uncomfortable," I said.
But things like manners, when one's dead,
hold little warmth. So I endured
the pumping pangs
of the vampire's grip, my throb blurred
through his thin fangs.

"Oh, why am I so cold?" I moaned,
my journey to the end postponed
with clammy hands and gummy fear.
I can't let slip
how many times in that first year
I bit my lip.

"Oh, why do you struggle?" I ask,
"Relax, the worst will soon be past.
Bright dark for you will loose its mask,

and then, at last,
another soul with me will bask
in the night, and the night is vast."

The Trick Is To Let Them Think What They Want To Think

JULEIGH HOWARD—HOBSON

They never find us anywhere.
We wait until dawn to return home,
but even if we didn't, they wouldn't know us.

Hate has made us twelve feet tall.
Fire breathing–
insatiable black beasts—preying
on innocents, ripping out their guts,
swallowing their beating hearts, whole.

The spawn of dark magic
and witches.
Scourge of lands.
Two headed evil.
They have no question

about these things that identify us
as monsters.

Without hesitation
They would kill us—all—no matter,
it's nonsense; we don't look like they think we do.
Even on full moons, we have one head…not two.

Treasure

DAVID C. KOPASKA—MERKEL

There is a door I may never open;
You know the story,
A loving husband, or,
At least he treats me kindly,
Showers me with gifts,
But, there's the door.

No reason given;
His house, his rules,
Bunch of corpsely brides,
I shouldn't wonder,
Hanging in the closet,
Desiccated corpses, or skeletons;
There's no odor of decay.

It's alright,
I'll find out soon enough,
Tonight, I'll straddle him by Moonrise.

As he fills me, so will She,
And I really hope he has murdered my predecessors;

A loving man would taste as sweet,
But the world's so few of those,
It'd be a shame,
It really would.

Mirrors Never Lie

C. H. Lindsay

Whispered words
of practiced seduction
punctuate the melody
of a Viennese Waltz.

His eyes mesmerize
with passion's promise,
Till they spin past a mirror. . .
and she's dancing alone.

Anguish

STEVEN F. CRANER

it hurts
needles
jagged as thorns that burn
with the alkaline poison of a cactus spine
insistent
long after the sliver has been removed
not the poignant wounds of a young child
whose whole world
may still be restored with a hug
a kiss on the cheek and
a bright bandaged badge of courage

it hurt long before I knew
what pain was
what to call such a friend who speaks
riddles in quiet interludes
destined to stir dark places that have no name
only the oily terror of wretched inadequacy

you know when you see it
we all know
often thinking if ignored
with rude overtones of bravado
it will simply slink away
to trouble instead the ones we despise
but
this gremlin plays no favorites
has no friend or foe
ravaging
with seemingly indiscriminate disdain
towards all of God's precious clay

I have pondered the nature of innocence
sought to hold its rainbow breath
with delicate instruments that work
in harmony with hand and heart
yet it dances
like oil upon a watery grave
vaporous in all of its wanderings
and yet
many a child has held its hand
while walking in gardens reserved
for their exchange
all to have that shattered
by the hungry callousness
of ignorance

I owe the demon this much
for long ago its rasping air
prodded me to seek
the Teacher
gentle unerring guide
with whom I learned to grant myself permission
while listening in anxious stillness
to the deepest cries of my heart

the Voice
throughout all of those harrowed years
has led me back
to the garden
to walk now and forever
hand in hand
with this joyously abundant life
tenderly embraced in a child's delight
lovingly upheld
while in this most gracious communion
of faithful family
and intimate friends

The Weredoodle of Wasatch Hollow

Alan J. Macfarlane

When the moon is full, and the clouds clear out
There are places you shouldn't be found.
On the moors;
In the woods;
Or a dark dead-end street,
Where the werewolf just might hunt you down.

But the danger you don't seem to hear much about
And some folks find hard to swallow
Is the one
All about
The fearsome (yet darling)
Weredoodle of ol' Wasatch Hollow.

"What's a weredoodle?" you might ask yourself
It's a legitimate question, indeed.
Part man
Part canine
But instead of a wolf
A doodle — the mixed poodle breed.

Wasatch Hollow is a quaint little place,
Salt Lake City's tree-lined hamlet,
With parks
And streetlamps
And brick bungalows —
As charming as neighborhoods get.

But no place is perfect and every utopia
Keeps skeletons in closets closed tight.
The kind
That embarrass
And destroy reputations
If the story creeps into the light.

The tale that's unique to dear Wasatch Hollow
Begins as they always do:
Just a guy
In a place
That he shouldn't have been
Scraping dog mess from the sole of his shoe.

Our friend's name is Buford Tom Talamahassy,
But Butch was his name around town.
A nickname
More common
For family dogs
But for him this name stuck around.

Butch sat just outside the King's English bookstore
Scraping poop off his shoe with a stick.
When he heard
An odd sound
From the back of an alley
A howl — most gruesome and sick.

Butch stood up straight and faced the darkness
And cocked his head to the right
To see
If he
Could better make out
What thing was disturbing the night.

The air became still, and it took on a chill
Like time stopped with nary a knell.
Then Butch
Stepped into
That damp, smelly alley
To see if he could offer some help.

Now let's just say that what happened in there
Wasn't good — and it left its mark.
And Butch
Now changed
And in a new way arranged
Limped home through the neighborhood park.

Let's skip ahead because nothing much happened
For a handful of crisp autumn days.
But when
The moon
Began its new cycle
A disturbance broke the malaise.

The first reports that came to the station
Picked up by Sheriff Costello
Were calls
And reports
About howling noises
And a vandalized patio pillow.

The neighbors discovered huge holes that were dug
All over their prim properties.
And oversized
Piles
Of canine excretion
Littered near gardens and trees.

Reports picked up of overturned trash cans
And chewed up morning newspapers
Everyone
Agitated
Annoyed and ticked off
Pointing fingers and blaming their neighbors.

But it was on the night of October 19th,
(the prime season of the witch)
The full moon
Was high
Illuminating the sky —
That's when tensions reached fever pitch.

Mrs. Grantooky was known all around
For her bed of huge prize-winning roses
Pink
And white
With billowing fragrance
That enchanted all passing-by noses.

She sat in her nightgown clipping coupons
For trash bags, and toothpaste, and Tide
When she
Thought she
Heard scratching and panting,
In her blue-ribbon garden outside.

"I hear you, you pervert," she yelled from the door
"I know who your parents are!"
"I'll call
"Costello
"He'll catch you, you creep!"
And her flashlight scanned over her yard.

And then it emerged from out of the night
And stood on its giant back paws.
It's eyes
glowed green
And it snarled and growled
And swiped at the air with its claws.

It drew in a breath, looked up at the moon
And reared back its curly, blond head
And howled,
(How it howled!)
So loud and so fearsome
It could have awakened the dead.

The beast looked straight at Mrs. Grantooky
And her gasp turned into a smile.
"Oh, my!
"You are
"The most adorable thing
"I've seen in a very long while."

“Just look at your coat, so shiny and blonde
“And that little white tuft on your chest.”
“It’s just...
“Oh my goodness…”
“Come here you sweet thing.”
“You’ll be my most honored guest.”

“Hold on, little sweetie” as she stepped inside
Away from the growling man-doodle
Then she
returned
With a beautiful pastry
Her famous homemade apple strudel.

The monster — half Butch, half cute goldendoodle
Just stood there in the porch light.
He whimpered,
Sniffed,
And wandered right over
Then gulped down the treat in one bite.

Now the once agitated but beautiful beast
Seemed appeased like never before.
He licked
His chops
And sniffed his behind
Then sprinted away on all fours.

So now when the full moon fills up the night sky
And front porches have plates with a strudel,
Don't fret,
It's safe,
Folks know how to prepare
For Butch, Wasatch Hollow's weredoodle.

Rotten Moonshine

C. H. Lindsay

There once was a zombie named Ross
whose leftover victims he'd toss.
They'd land in the still
and turn into swill
'till all of his neighbors were sauce.

Part III: Expeditions

Novelettes

Good Fences

Julie Frost

The realtor gestures over the fence to the neglected, overgrown, old cemetery fifty feet from the side of the house. “At least the neighbors are quiet.”

“Does that joke work with anyone?” I ask.

She has the grace to look ashamed of herself. “Not really.”

I eye the place. She has a point, as hackneyed as the joke was. Quiet suits me just now; I need it after the chaos and clamor of IEDs and screaming and gunfire. The house itself sits off the road a piece, and is what’s charitably known as a “fixer-upper.” But it’s on a good-sized piece of property where I can run a few sheep if I want—and Tripod, the unimaginatively-named three-legged dog I’d brought back from my last tour in Iraq, will have room to roam.

“This one’s been on the market awhile, and the seller is motivated, Joe,” she says. “You could probably get him to come down a few thousand on the price.”

I think about it for a few more moments before nodding decisively. "I like it. I want it. Let's make it happen."

±Δ±

And we do. It takes far too long, and the paperwork is a nightmare, but I finally get to move into the house of my—well, maybe not dreams. But a place I'm happy to settle into and call "home," in a way I haven't called anyplace home in several years.

On our first night, I sit on the sofa in front of the fire, with a celebratory Jack Daniels in my hand and Tripod draped across my lap. He isn't a small dog, and he's short-haired, with half-floppy ears and white fur. He's got a black mask, and another pair of spots splotch his back. He seems to know exactly what I'd rescued him from, and he's damned grateful, even though we hadn't been able to save his left hind leg. I play with his ears, and his tail thumps on the cushions.

"Well, fella. I can get used to this. How about you?" His tail thumps harder, and we stare companionably into the flames—flames contained by the grate and the screen, flames that won't jump out. This is part of my desensitization therapy, and the cold sweat I started with has been subsumed by the fact that this fire is under control and not, you know, hurting anyone.

The sound begins as a low, snarling wail at the edge of my hearing, and Tripod's head comes up as he shrinks against me. The wail builds to a shriek that leaves my ears ringing, then dies away. "The hell. . .?" So much for the neighbors being quiet.

And then it starts again.

Tripod dives off the couch and stuffs himself between it and the wall, shivering. I growl with annoyance—not at him, never at him, but at the ungodly noise that scared him—and get up, grabbing my pump-action shotgun and a handful of shells from the closet. I shut the light off before stalking out the back door; no sense in silhouetting myself against it and making myself more of a target. My head jerks to the right, toward the graveyard.

A deep fog loops and swirls inside the fence—but only inside the fence. It has its own weather system going in there, and things fly through it, or seem to. They're the same color as the fog, but denser, somehow, and move with purpose. Chills skitter up and down my spine and raise the hairs on my arms and the back of my neck. My stomach lurches with sudden nausea. Whatever's happening, it's not natural. That wail never stops, building and descending, building and descending.

I tighten my grip on the shotgun and creep toward the cemetery to get a better look, using shadows from the big trees in the yard as cover. Stopping behind an old elm just outside the fence, I poke my head around, briefly, before yanking it back. But the things in the cemetery don't notice, so I look again, not pulling away. Now that I'm closer, I can hear a murmuring through the wail, voices just under the threshold of intelligible. Does this go on every night? No wonder the previous owner had been so desperate to get out from under this thing. It's spooky and *not right*, and goose bumps pebble my skin as my gut roils.

I twitch violently when one of the things looks directly at me. It's vaguely female, and it turns a sharp and knowing glance right at my face before swooping back into the fog and disappearing. The voices get louder, until I can make out phrases and sentences amid the shriek that brought me out into the chilly evening, with the full moon shining down on all of it.

A creature lurches out of the fog and hits the fence, and I recoil. It's manlike, but huge and hulking, at least a foot taller than my own six-two. I'm surprised the fence holds it back, honestly, but it can't even reach between the iron bars, an invisible barrier preventing it. It sees me and humps its shoulders, growing larger and shifting its shape. It smells horrific, like rotting meat, and old dirt, and painful death.

Right before my horrified eyes, it turns into a bull. With no skin.

It throws back its head and bellows, and I can see the muscles and tendons *move*. Almost without thinking, I bring my shotgun up and fire. The buckshot hits—I can't miss at that distance and I see it connect—but it has absolutely no effect on the creature. It doesn't even bleed. But it glares malevolently at me before letting out another shriek and staggering back into the mist.

I lean against the elm, heart pounding, and slide to the ground. Wondering if the moderate PTSD from my last tour in Iraq has turned into a full-blown psychosis, I very carefully set the shotgun aside. "Things like that don't exist. Do they?"

"Things like what, honey? That critter?" The girlish voice with the Southern accent makes me jerk my head up, and I make a strangled sound. Apparently, the Powers That Be have decided that my night hasn't been weird or traumatic enough, because they've sent a see-through apparition wearing a long, corseted dress straight out of *Gone With the Wind* to sit on the fence. She holds a closed parasol, and a truly remarkable hat covered with flowers and stuffed birds perches on her head. "Oh, he's real, all right, and quite unhappy about it, too."

My mouth moves, but no words come out, just an undignified squeak.

"He's trapped inside here, we all are," she prattles on. "Mostly it don't make no nevermind, it's a nice enough place, little run down, but doesn't he make a ruckus about it."

I finally make my tongue work. "You're a ghost."

"Why, yes, honey. What was your first clue?"

I wave my hand. "Oh, just. Everything." I've lost it. Clearly. If I was still sane, I would not be talking to a *ghost* in a *cemetery* about a noisy *Thing* that turned into a skinless *bull*. I should probably call my therapist. I have him on speed dial.

"You're lookin' a bit peaked. You should make yourself a nice cup of tea and have a lie-down." She nods decisively. "Tea makes everything better. I miss it, I do declare."

"Do you." My voice is faint. My whole body is faint, really. I can't feel my face. "And what kind do you recommend?"

"This time of night, chamomile, definitely. Don't know if it'll help you sleep through *that*, but it might do." The screams from the Thing still haven't stopped. "Oh, bother, bother, bother," she says over her shoulder. "Do shut up, you are being absolutely ridiculous."

"Please tell me that works."

She makes a face. "Not often. Sorry, sugar."

I rest my elbows on my bent knees and bury my face in my arms. "The neighbors were supposed to be quiet. I just got back from a war. The last thing I need is more screaming."

"Buck up, darlin'. He only does it at night." She sounds unbearably cheerful. "You can sleep in the daytime, right?"

"I don't sleep well at the best of times, let alone when a monster is screaming like the damned fifty feet from my back door. I'm not sure switching to daylight will help. And once I get a real job. . ." My head comes up. "How long have you been doing this, Miss—?"

"Laurel Hines. And I'd say, oh. . .century and a half? Something like that, anyhow, you lose track after a while. Critter was here before me."

"Joe Hawes." I'm introducing myself to a ghost. My therapist will have a field day with this. "Recently separated from the US Marine Corps, and unsure what I want to do with the rest of my life." I'm only twenty-eight. You wouldn't think it'd be that hard. You'd be wrong.

"At least you have a rest-a your life. Could be worse."

The Thing's screeching picks that moment to increase in pitch and volume again. "I suppose I could be living right on top of that instead of next door to it. What does it want, anyway?"

"Nearly as we can tell, it was grave-robbed a few decades back, and ornery over it. It wants outta the cemetery so it can hunt down the stolen treasure and exact revenge or some such claptrap." She snorts. It's a remarkably ladylike sound. "I expect whatever treasure there was is long gone by now."

"Mmph. And what would it take," I ask, ultra-casually, "to let it out of there?" So I can get some damn rest.

She points her parasol at me. "It's a real bad idea, sweet pea, is what it is, so don't you be entertainin' thoughts such as that. We in here, we're already dead, and it can't hurt us. It can hurt the living right enough, and has done to a few poor souls foolhardy enough to brave this place of a night."

I frown a little. "What about you? Are you trapped in there too?"

She shrugs. "Got nowhere else to go."

I'm not religious, by any stretch of the imagination, but— "What about Heaven? Follow the light? Isn't that what you're supposed to do?"

Her mouth twists. "If I was gonna go there, I think I'd've already gone. This beats the alternative, I guess."

She has a point, but that doesn't mean I like it. Something in my expression must tell her that, because she holds up a hand. "Don't go doin' nothin' foolish-like on my account, now. I'm safe and comfy here, we all are, except that—" The Thing makes a particularly loud noise, while her voice goes faded and watery. "And it doesn't count. Right?"

Maybe it doesn't, but the screams I'm hearing aren't from it, anymore, they're from Burchard and Daniels and Robison as their Humvee catches an incendiary IED and blows up. I watch in horror as it skids off the road in slow motion, flips over, and bursts into flames. They're caught inside, and no one can get near it. I try, and smarter people than me drag me back with my clothes smoking and my hands burned. The fire extinguishers do no good at all, the bastard insurgents used phosphorus on this one and it burns hot and steady, and we're helpless. . .

"Joe? Joseph?" Laurel's voice comes from far away, and I blink back to the present, huddled against the tree with my arms over my head. "Are you all right?"

I shake my head, swallowing hard. "I don't. . .don't like it when people are trapped."

"We aren't 'people,' as such, and that critter isn't either. No need to fuss yourself about us."

There's every need, but that's my issue, not hers. I stagger to my feet, picking up the shotgun by the barrel. My knees don't particularly want to hold me up, but I make them. "I should—" I wave vaguely toward the house.

"You do that, darlin'. Was nice meeting you." She smiles; it's a lovely expression. "Don't be a stranger. The critter only comes out at night, but the rest of us aren't so bound. And it's nice to talk to new folks."

I nod jerkily. "Be seeing you."

I'm not even sure how I get back into the house, but I do. Kicking off my boots on my way to the bedroom, I whistle up Tripod. He creeps out from behind the couch and licks my hand before hopping up onto the bed with me and curling up against my stomach.

The thing doesn't stop screaming until dawn, and wrapping a pillow around my head is wholly inadequate for drowning it out. I finally fall into a fitful sleep as daylight slips in through the blinds.

±Δ±

I wake up after noon, logy and heavy-limbed. My mouth tastes like a plague-ridden wharf rat crawled inside and died, and I grimace and haul myself into the bathroom to brush my teeth. My face in the mirror is haggard, dark circles shadowing my eyes and lines bracketing my mouth. I look fifteen years older than I am, and I scrub up with a washcloth and decide not to bother shaving.

Tripod is much happier, bouncing around while I scoop kibble into his bowl and charging outside when I open the back door. In daylight, the cemetery is just a cemetery, kind of forlorn and empty, but not actively malevolent. Maybe everything last night was a bad dream or some kind of trauma-induced hallucination? It wouldn't be the first time.

I get a pot of coffee going and call my therapist to make an appointment. He's had a cancellation and can get me in at two. I take a quick shower so I'm not completely unpresentable.

Dr. Mendenhall blinks when I walk into his office and sit heavily. "Rough night, Joe?"

I huff out a breath. "You could say that." I've just about convinced myself that I fell asleep in front of the fire, and the whole thing was a nightmare, so I couch it in those terms. Mendenhall takes careful notes, making encouraging noises in appropriate places, and he sits back when I'm done, tapping his pen on his teeth. I tilt my head. "What do you think, Doc?"

"I think your subconscious is trying to find a way to deal with everything that's happened. It's given you a distressed damsel and a monster to fight."

I snort. "She seems to think I'm the distressed one."

"Well. You felt pretty helpless in Iraq, a lot of the time, especially after that last incident." The one that had sent me stateside with a medical discharge. "But now that you're back home and at loose ends, you might be looking for the next mission, the next battle. One you can actually win." His mouth twists. "Have you figured out what you're going to do now that you're separated from the Corps?"

"Not yet." I hadn't planned on being separated from the Corps. This is a problem. "I'm still thinking about it. I'd like to, I don't know, keep a few sheep on that piece of property, or something." Although considering how Tripod reacted to the screaming, I'm not sure that sheep are such a great idea. Tripod has actual sense, while sheep are damned silly creatures. They'd probably run themselves to death, or beat themselves bloody on the fence. And then I realize that I'm thinking like it *wasn't* a nightmare and shake myself out of that mindset. "In the meantime, I've got home repairs to make."

"Something to do with your hands. That's always a good thing." He nods. "How are you adjusting otherwise?"

"Not bad, you know, still a little twitchy. Tripod helps. He's a good dog."

"Pets are often useful in situations like this. Are you taking the meds still?"

"Yessir, although I'm not sure how much good they're doing."

"We'll wean you off them gradually and see how that goes, okay? For now, keep taking them on your regular schedule." He taps the pen on my file this time. "Any other concerns, any incidents you want to tell me about?"

"No, sir, not really. This one was just weird enough that I thought I should see you today."

"It wasn't a bad idea. But I think you're just trying to come to grips with all the trauma and changes in your life, and this is your mind's way of dealing. It's not a bad thing, necessarily."

By this time I'm pretty sure that the whole thing was a figment of my distraught imagination. Who talks to ghosts, anyway? No one, is who. Even the people on those ghost hunter shows don't normally hear anything until they get their equipment back to the studio.

Yeah. It was a nightmare. Had to be.

"Thanks, doc. I feel better." And I do. If it's just my subconscious screwing with me, well, I can deal with that.

What if it's not? asks a niggling voice in the back of my head.

Shut up, I tell it.

±Λ±

I spend the rest of the day stripping wallpaper, which is more tiring than it sounds even for a big tough Marine. By the time I sit down in front of the TV to an all-the-meats pizza delivered from a local joint and a well-earned bottle of beer, I feel like I've run a marathon. But I've got a sense of accomplishment that offsets the exhaustion, and I share a slice with Tripod, who's stayed out from underfoot all day and deserves a reward too.

The scream makes me choke on a mouthful of pizza. Tripod yelps and dives behind the couch again, and it occurs to me that this time, I'm definitely wide awake. If he can hear it too, it's not a hallucination. Right? I leap to my feet and stalk outside, without the shotgun. The same creepy-ass fog swirls around the cemetery, and the same shapes flit in and out of it. I stomp up to the fence and shout, "Shut up! Can't a guy get some decent rest around here?"

Laurel flies over and perches in front of me. "Now, sugar. No need for all the hoo-raw."

"Tell *it* that." I gesture at the mist. "I've been working very hard all damn day, and all I want is to sit down in front of the TV, watch a mindless action flick, and veg for awhile."

"I don't know what any of that is, but he is kinda noisy, yeah."

She seems awfully offhanded about it. "I guess you're used to it by now."

"I've learned to ignore it. It's just noise."

It's noise that gets right down into the insanity center of my brain. Putting my hands over my ears doesn't block it out in the slightest. "How do I let the damn thing out so it'll *stop*?"

"Now, honey, I done told you that's a terrible idea. You're better off just drinking yourself insensible and sleeping through it."

"Right, that's healthy." I growl. "Can't you talk some sense into it?"

"We've tried." She twirls the parasol like a baton. "It's no use."

"I can't live like this, Laurel." I clench my fist. "And I can't afford to move. At least now I know why the previous owners were so anxious to sell."

"No one stays in that house for long. You've got all my sympathies, Joe."

"I'm glad of that. I am. But they don't really help."

"It's been like this for longer'n I've been here."

My jaw tightens. "Well, maybe it's time it changed."

"Joe. . ."

"What is that Thing, Laurel? Has it got a name?"

She looks uneasy, or as uneasy as a specter can look, anyway. "He says he's a draugr, whatever that is, when we can get him to say anything at all. That, and he's angry about gettin' his treasure stolen. We ask him what difference it makes, since he's dead an' all, but that only makes him more irate."

"It's a starting point. And if I'm going to be up anyway, I think it's time for me to do some research. Does he have an actual name? Was he human once?"

"Jorgen Petersson. But, Joe—"

"Thank you, Laurel. I'll see you tomorrow night,

probably."

I spin on my heel and walk back to the house, shoulders stiff, and flump into the chair in front of the computer. First thing to do is search for "draugr," which gives me all kinds of disturbing results that I decide not to look at too closely, after a preliminary glance.

Then I look up Jorgen Petersson, my town, and put in a date parameter of between 300 and 150 years in the past. "Oh, isn't that interesting," I mutter. "Weren't you a big deal back in the day, Mr. Big Scary Monster." He'd been one of the town elders, and he'd died under mysterious circumstances, which I figure is par for the course. His will stipulated that he be buried with most of his "treasure" in a mound outside of town, because he was a bitter old bastard who hated his relatives and didn't think they deserved any of it. Later, a church had been built at the site and the graveyard situated there.

Later still, there were reports of people breaking into the cemetery and stealing stuff—sometimes whole bodies—from the graves. One of the first places hit was Petersson's mound. Some of the items had been recovered, but by no means all of them, and that was when odd things started happening. People died in their sleep with horrified expressions and crushed chests, their houses ransacked and torn apart and their blood drained. Someone finally put two and two together when they discovered that one of the dead guys was one of the thieves. Panicked, the townsfolk tried to find Petersson's other possessions, but there was no way they could recover every last piece.

Deaths kept occurring and they eventually called in an exorcist. He died, too, but not before warding the cemetery so nothing could get out ever again.

And it's apparently worked, for all this time. What really surprises me is that my house is still standing. Why someone hadn't torn it down long ago, like they had the church, is a question for the ages. But here it is and I'm stuck with it. I scrub a hand over my face and sigh.

Tripod creeps out from behind the sofa and lays his head on my lap. "So, basically what I've got here is a pissed-off undead guy who's mad because people stole his crap after he was done using it. Awesome." And still the screaming goes on. And on. And on.

"What am I gonna do, Tripod? We can't live like this. I wonder—" I think about it for a few minutes. None of the people who'd taken Petersson's treasure are still alive. Hell, some of them are buried in that selfsame graveyard, and it's probably no picnic for them. But maybe if I let him out. . .

"Maybe if I let him out, he'll calm the hell down, once he realizes that no one here even remembers who he is." Tripod droops his ears and whines up at me, putting a paw in my lap. "No one likes being trapped." And maybe I really am asleep, and he's a hallucination or a nightmare, and if I turn him loose, I'll be rid of him for good. The screams, after all, are eerily reminiscent of the screams coming from that Humvee. Maybe this is one long delusion and I never bought a house at all. Isn't that a pleasant thought. I shove it away, not sure which would be better.

Of course, I have no idea how to actually take the wards down. This will require more research. But I look at the clock and realize that the sun will be up in another hour, so I shut the computer off and get ready for bed.

Just as I lay my head on my pillow, the screaming, blessedly, stops. Before I know it, I'm out.

±A±

A nightmare jerks me out of slumber the next day, gasping and sweating. Most of it slides away before I can remember it, but the smell of burning metal and flesh fills my nostrils and the heat of the flaming Humvee sears my hands for a brief instant before I come fully awake. I know I won't get back to sleep, not after that, so I ignore my wallpaper and delve back into the computer. There are a few articles on taking wards down, but most of them involve knowing how they went up in the first place. That's information I don't have.

So I wander out to the cemetery, Tripod at my heels, and examine the wrought-iron fence that surrounds it. It's square—like, perfectly square—and, sighting along it, I notice that it's set along compass lines. The sides line up with north, south, east, and west, and sigils and runes are branded into the corner posts at top, center, and bottom.

From the research, breaking sigils is a good way to dispel a ward. "That's a starting place, anyway," I say to Tripod, and he wags his tail as we go back inside.

I'm not completely stupid. I don't want to let Petersson out without having some kind of self-protection. If the runes guard the cemetery, maybe they'll guard me too. I take a pad of paper and a pen back out and painstakingly copy all of them down.

Back inside, I grab a marker and write the runes from the northwest corner on my left arm, top on my shoulder, middle at my elbow, and bottom at my wrist. I repeat the operation at hips, knees, and ankles for the southeast and southwest runes, then swap hands and inscribe the northeast runes on my right arm. That one is more difficult, because I'm not used to writing with my left hand, but it'll do.

I should probably eat before I attempt this, so I make a quick sandwich and scarf it down. "Here goes nothing." Grabbing a rasp and a flashlight from my toolbox, I head back out, closing the door on Tripod's crestfallen face.

Just as the sun drops below the horizon, that eerie fog goes to swirling around, starting at the mound in the northwest corner of the cemetery where Petersson is buried. That by-now-familiar low wail builds to a shriek, and the skinless bull slams into the fence right beside me. It's pretty solid for a hallucination. I try not to think about the fact that it might not be one. Illusion and reality are morphing together in a pretty disturbing way, and I wonder if the drugs have anything to do with that. "Keep your shirt on. I'm working on it," I say.

"Working on what, sugar?" Laurel is suddenly there, leaning on the rail and eyeing my preparations worriedly as the Thing stumbles back into the mist. "You're not thinking about turning the critter loose, are you?"

"Him, and all of you," I growl. "I don't like the idea of

anyone being trapped, not him, not you. I know you say you don't mind, but dammit, I do."

"This is a terrible idea, Joe. Please don't do it."

"If I don't, Petersson will drive me crazy. Hell, not even Mr. Rogers would want him as a neighbor." I set the rasp against the topmost sigil on the northeast corner and scrape at it. "I value my sanity."

"And when he starts killing folks, what'll that do to your sanity, huh?"

"He won't. No one's left who stole his stuff." The rune lets go with a little pop and sizzle and scent of ozone, and I jerk back for a moment as the corresponding rune on my left shoulder flares with low-level heat. Huh. But it doesn't hurt, so I set to work on the next one down. This one goes faster, now that I know what I'm doing. Same effect: pop, sizzle, ozone, heat.

Petersson's roars grow impossibly louder as each successive rune breaks. "Should've brought earplugs," I mutter, setting to work on the last corner post. As the final sigil dies, Petersson goes blessedly silent and Laurel, who's followed along, shrinks into herself. "Well. That's torn it."

I sit back on my heels. "Has it? Can you get out?"

Her brow creases. "I—No. No, I can't." A smile. "Well, that's a relief."

"Crap. It should've worked, why didn't it. . ." I stand up and examine the rest of the fence. Exactly midway between the corners, the first center post I come to is also runed. I take a close look at them, and they're the same as the ones

I've already broken. "Aha."

"Joe, please!" Laurel looks frantically over her shoulder. "You don't know what you're letting loose."

"He's trapped. You're trapped. Maybe if I can set you free, I'll be less trapped." Issues, me? Nah.

Okay, maybe. I'll talk to Doc Mendenhall about them at our next appointment. In the meantime, I'm *doing something*, taking control of the situation, and it feels *good.* I couldn't get my comrades out of that burning vehicle, but I can sure as hell get Laurel out of this cemetery, along with everyone else in it. *If she's real*, a voice snickers in my head. I tell it to shut up, making the rounds of the fence again, and Laurel lets out a gasp as the final sigil does its pop-sizzle-ozone routine.

Petersson lets out another roar, but there's a triumphant note in it this time. The skinless bull stampedes out of the fog and through the fence like it's not solid, or he's not solid, or something—but he's sure as hell solid enough to knock me on my ass on his way by. I'm not sure a hallucination can do that.

He doesn't stop, though. "You're welcome!" I holler after his disappearing form, sitting up and dusting myself off amid a stench of rotting flesh.

Laurel flits through the fence and huddles beside me as the fog dissipates. "Oh, Joe. What've you done?"

"Freed him. Freed you. Maybe now we can all get some damn rest."

Her voice is forlorn. "I don't think any of us will rest

ever again."

‡Δ‡

Tripod's not hiding behind the couch when I come in, and I finally get a night's sleep unplagued by nightmares. When I wake up, actually refreshed, I feel better than I have for a long time. I guess setting someone free made my subconscious happy. I turn on the TV for the morning news programs while my coffeemaker burbles in the background.

"—crushed to death last night, his blood drained. Police are baffled and asking the public's help." My head snaps around. "We've never seen injuries like this," the sheriff says. "It's uncanny. There's no sign of forced entry, and all his doors and windows were locked, but Dr. Mendenhall was obviously murdered."

The shot switches back to the studio. The reporter's eyes are wide, and I don't blame her. Mine are too. It's a sleepy town, really, and not used to things like this. "His house was ransacked, but relatives say that nothing was obviously missing. Police have no motive in the killing."

Reaching blindly for the remote, I shut the TV off and sit down. I liked Mendenhall, he was a good therapist, and now. . .

The timing on this can't possibly be a coincidence. I guess that means that Petersson isn't a hallucination after all. I rake my fingers through my hair, at a loss—

Then run out the door to the cemetery. "Laurel! Are you here? Laurel!"

She's fainter in the daylight, but she's there, all right, sitting on a headstone—her headstone—with her chin in her hand, contemplating the distance. "Hello, Joe," she says without turning her head. "You get that rest you were craving?"

"What did you call Petersson? A draugr?"

"It's what he called himself, anyway. Why?" She looks at me, finally. "Did something happen last night?"

"My therapist was murdered. Crushed to death and his blood drained." I feel faint, and I lean on the headstone beside her. "What have I done." It's not a question.

"I don't like to say I told you so, but I surely did, didn't I." That's not a question either.

I swallow hard. I'm a Marine, I've lost plenty of people, but this—

This hits me harder than normal. Maybe because Mendenhall wasn't a soldier, maybe because I thought I left all that behind when I got back stateside, maybe because I feel directly responsible for his death. Even in Iraq, I'd never caused an innocent to die. "What a mess."

"You ain't wrong about that, sugar."

"How do I fix it?"

"Trap it back in the cemetery, for starters. Kill it, somehow, maybe." She spins her parasol, frowning a little. "Though how you kill something that's already dead is a puzzlement, isn't it."

I make a noise halfway between a growl and a whine. "I guess this means more research. And I guess next time I'll pay more attention to the research I've already done." And maybe I'll start trusting my senses when they tell me something terrible is standing right there.

"Be best for everyone if you do, honey." For a ghost, she's damned expressive.

"Yes, thank you so much for not rubbing it in." A sigh. "For what it's worth, I'm sorry I didn't listen to you."

The severe line of her eyebrows softens, just a little. "Oh, well, it happens. But I hope you can fix it, Joe. This deal is all manner of bad."

"Tell me about it." I trudge back into the house and flop into the computer chair. Tripod sits next to me and lays his head on my lap, and I play with his ears. "Well, boy, isn't this a cluster-foxtrot. At least I wrote the runes down, so I think I can duplicate them. Now it's a matter of trapping the Thing and then getting rid of it permanently."

Clacking at the keyboard. Banging my head on it. "I have to cut its head off, burn the body, and then dump the ashes in the sea?" I'm hundreds of miles from "sea." I shudder. Not to mention the fact that I don't much like fire.

"Maybe the lake, then."

The voice over my shoulder startles me, and I let out a yell and flail a little. "Laurel!"

"I didn't mean to startle you. But I ain't been outta the graveyard since I was buried and thought I'd visit, now that I can."

"Well, you nearly gave me a heart attack." I wave a hand. "But welcome to my humble abode." She looks around, frowning a little, and I realize that the place is a middle-ofrenovations mess. "I know it's not much right now, but I'm remodeling. 'Scuse the clutter?"

"Eh, I'm not seeing what it is, but what it can be. It's a beautiful place, Joe, or will be when you're done." She waves her parasol. "I was more looking at—this thing. And that thing." The computer, and the TV. If she hasn't been out of the graveyard, she's probably never seen them.

I try to think of analogies she'd understand. "Well, this one. . . is kind of a library I don't need to leave the house to get to. And the other thing is, like, entertainment in my living room. Plays, sort of?"

"Modern society's turned into a buncha homebodies, then. Not sure I approve of such, but to each his own." Her brow creases. "Did you find anything out?"

"How to kill it. Sort of. I guess I need to get it back into the cemetery somehow first." I rub my forehead. "And hope it doesn't murder anyone else in the meantime."

She nods at the Marine sword hanging over the mantle. "Do you know how to use that? It might be handy for cutting its head off. I don't know that it's got any weapons but what it is, y'know?"

"It's more ceremonial than anything else. I'm not even sure how sharp it is."

She gives me a look. "Best you find out, sugar. You already saw how effective your funny-lookin' musket wasn't." She has a point, and I pull the sword off its mount and unsheathe it. "Oh," she breathes, "that's lovely."

I test my thumb on the edge. It's not nearly sharp

enough to whack the head off an undead monster. "I guess the principles for sharpening it would be the same as for sharpening a knife," I muse. I've got a whetstone lying around, and it doesn't take me long to find it in my toolbox. Long strokes up and down the blade, and the motion is soothing, in a way. "Has it come back yet?"

"No. I don't know where it is."

"Ugh." I want this to be over. "If it's not in its mound, then where would it be?"

"Could be anywhere, Joe. You turned it loose. You can't be surprised when it wants to stretch its legs for a spell."

"Suppose not." Doesn't mean I'm not grouchy about it, though. "I'll go into town tonight and see what I can scare up. It might not be expecting real opposition."

"Don't reckon it will be." She tips her head. "Be careful, Joe. I like you and wouldn't want you to join us in an untimely fashion."

"Do my best," I answer wryly. Just the same, I go ahead and load the shotgun and an extra box of shells into the pickup truck, and strap on the shoulder holster for my (legally concealed) 9mm Ruger. It never pays to be under-armed when you might be going into battle with a monster.

±A±

My first stop in town is Mendenhall's house, and I park on the street and just stare at it, with its yellow police tape across the door. Why him, what did he do to attract the Thing's attention? Frowning, it takes me a few moments to realize that this is one of the older houses—there's even a sign on the knee-high white picket fence saying it's a historic home, and the date when it was built.

And by whom.

Oh.

"You nasty old sonofabitch," I mutter. "Just because you lived here two hundred years ago doesn't mean you get to take over now and murder someone to do it." My jaw tightens. "I'm sorry, Doc."

But if Petersson didn't find what he'd been looking for, that means he'll probably go looking again tonight. Where else would he go?

Anything not buried with him would have ended up with relatives, and then as they died off, antique stores, probably. Main Street has several, so I shift the pickup into gear and head that way.

The deeper into downtown I get, however, the more disturbed I am. I slam on the brakes a couple of times to avoid hitting dogs, and once a person who seems to have no idea where she is or what she's doing. Someone else comes out of a house and takes charge of her, and I continue on, finding a parking space and shutting down. I get out of the truck, my hand reaching halfway to my Ruger but not drawing it. Yet.

The street is eerily empty of people, although I can hear human screams, laughter, and crying coming from several quarters. A man bursts out of an alleyway and crashes into me, spilling us both to the sidewalk. He grabs my jacket. "Did you see it? Did you?" He glares wildly over his shoulder, screams at nothing I can see, and scrambles to his feet, scampering away.

Screw it, my gun's in my hand now, and I stop short outside one of the antique shops. The window lies in shards all over the ground, and a glance at the shattered china inside tells me that something very like a tornado went through the place. Or maybe a skinless bull. I holler a cautious "Hello?" but no one answers. Stepping inside, I wander through, but I've got no way of telling if anything's gone.

A low scraping sound makes me jerk my head toward the cash register, and I creep that way and peek over the counter. An older woman lies sprawled on the floor, obviously and horribly dead. Her expression is one of stark terror, and her lifeless, clawed hands push at—

That is the biggest fucking cat I've ever seen. It's sitting on her chest, which is crushed nearly to the floor, and I'd swear it *smiles* up at me before hopping casually off and dissolving into smoke. I snap off a shot, but you can't shoot something that's not there. I stumble back outside.

A fight spills out of a bar a few doors down, people clawing and kicking and punching each other for no apparent reason. The whole town's gone crazy. I run back to my pickup, stuffing the Ruger back in its holster and fumbling for my keys. Leaping behind the wheel, I get the motor started and peel away from the curb, narrowly missing some of the fighters as their scrum expands into the road. If I'm hallucinating, so's the rest of the town.

I race home as fast as I can go, not worried about getting pulled over for speeding. If the sheriff hasn't gone nuts himself, he's got his hands full. Screeching to a stop beside my front door, I sprint inside and slam it shut, shooting the deadbolt home with a quick flick of my wrist. I lean my back on the door and slide to the floor, panting, as Tripod dances up to my side, happy to see me.

I hug him, hard, gladder than I can say that whatever Petersson did to the town, he apparently spared my dog and my house. I bury my face in Tripod's shoulder fur, and he leans on me, tail thumping.

"Looks like things are pear-shaped, sugar." Laurel's voice startles me, and I nearly draw down on her before I remember myself and pull my hand out of my jacket, empty.

I shake my head. "I'd say things are about as bad as they can be, but a war zone taught me that the universe has a way of laughing in your face when you say things like that, and doing its level best to prove you wrong."

She sits beside me. Tripod is puzzled when he reaches over to lick her and can't, but accepts it philosophically and goes back to resting against me. I almost wish I was a dog. Life would be simpler.

"What're you gonna do, then?" she asks.

"I don't know." My voice shakes. "I unleashed that Thing and now—"

"Now you gotta chain it back up." She nods. "The right bait'll bring it back to the cemetery. Then you can bind it in there, anyway."

I wrench my brain into a semblance of working. "I

need to prep for it, first. Get the runes back on the corner and center posts. I think, if I just leave one undone, it'll go in without realizing it's walking into a trap."

Laurel frowns. "Once it does, though, you're gonna have to do that last rune lickety-split. It'd go bad for you if it escaped before you could."

"Maybe just the last line on the last rune."

She consults some sort of inner knowledge, her expression going blank for a moment. "That would work." I feel a chill through my jacket as she lays her hand on my arm. "Do be careful, though, Joe. The critter is dangerous."

"I know," I answer grimly. But once it's trapped, I can decide how to dispatch it.

I think.

±A±

With no time to lose, I grab my cordless metal etching tool, my snake flashlight, and the pad I wrote the runes down on. I painstakingly copy them onto the correct posts while Laurel watches over my shoulder. Just before I do the last one, she flits into the cemetery. "Laurel, what're you doing?"

She shrugs a little. "This is my home, Joe. I don't want to be trapped outside."

That makes me blink. "Trapped out—" I supposed there are different ways of being trapped, and it's her decision, although I don't like it much. My brow creases. "Okay." Hopefully, once this is over for good, the graveyard won't have to be warded anymore and she can come and go as she pleases. I finish all but the last line on the last sigil and leave the etcher right where it is for easy access. I'll only have one chance to do this right.

I hop the fence and make my way to Petersson's mound. There's a giant rent in the side of it, but it looks like whatever escaped accomplished the feat long ago. "They quit tryin' to close it back up over half a century back," Laurel says. "Since it wasn't any use."

I grunt, duck my head, and go in. The interior is illuminated by flickering light from nowhere I can see, and I shiver. It's filled with things, furniture and knick-knacks from a bygone age. I frown, wondering what I can take that'll get Petersson's attention. . .

My gaze is drawn to a doll sitting in a miniature chair on the dresser, surrounded by unlit candles. Clearly, there's a story there, and just as clearly the doll is something he prizes, even though it doesn't look particularly valuable for its own sake. I pick it up and take it outside.

Laurel nods with appreciation. "Aren't you clever. That's just the thing to bring him running, sugar."

"I hope so." I jump back out and stand beside the uncompleted rune with the doll in one hand and the etcher in the other. Waiting.

It doesn't take long. An angry roar cascades from the semi-darkness, along with a thunder of hooves. My eyes widen when I see a gray horse with no ears or tail galloping straight toward me, teeth bared. I wonder hysterically how it even moves, because its back is obviously, horribly broken, but that's all I have time for before it slams into me and sends me crashing into the fence.

My head cracks against one of the posts, and the breath is knocked clean out of me. But I can't just lie here. *Get up, get up, get up*, my brain screams at me, *before that Thing has another go at you and you end up like Mendenhall or that poor antique store lady.*

Petersson howls again. I've barely scrambled to my knees before he hits me once more, from behind this time, and I sprawl onto my face, my hands convulsively clutching the doll and the tool. Giant hooves smash onto my back, and I have no idea how it's not busted in half by the impact. I brace, and roll, and it misses its second strike, squealing with rage.

Well, this was a terrible idea, I think muzzily. What had the plan been? Had there even been a plan? Surely I went into this with a plan. . .

Doll. The doll. Something with the damned doll, what—

Oh. Dumbass. I roll again, making it upright this time, and fling the doll with all my might into the graveyard. "Go fetch," I wheeze, and, for a wonder, it does.

The post. Where's the fucking post? I'm hurt and disoriented, but if I don't finish the sigil, Petersson will come out and finish *me*. I catch sight of the flashlight on the ground, and if it's where I left it then it should be right in front of the center post. Next time I do the last sigil on a corner post. Easier to find. I'm free-associating, but I'm also crawling determinedly in that direction.

I get to it, there's the sigil, one more line, oops, better turn the etcher on first, that works better, and Petersson's charging out of the fog again, this time as the skinned bull, and I finish the rune just as he hits the fence—

And bounces off, screaming.

I collapse onto the ground in sheer relief with an arm over my eyes. At least Petersson is back where he belongs now, and no more people in town will die. Breathing in pained gasps—I'm pretty sure I've got cracked ribs—I notice that the sigils I drew on myself are uncomfortably warm. I lift my right arm, and the runes are glowing red. "That's new," I mutter. It occurs to me that they probably saved my life, somehow.

I'm tired, and it's not over yet. But it's over for now. I'm not sure I can even make it back to the house. I suppose I should probably try. My entire body hurts. I take a couple of tries and jack myself to my feet, staggering and stumbling and tripping over irregularities in the ground, but I eventually make it to the back door, shove it open, and collapse onto the floor.

Tripod bellies up to me and licks my face, whining, and I reach a shaking hand out and pet him. "It's okay, boy. It's okay." Even the unbearable shrieking from the cemetery isn't enough to keep me conscious, and blackness carries me down.

±Δ±

I wake up stiff and cold and aching on the floor with Tripod curled against my stomach. He lifts his head when I moan, and his tail thumps against my leg. “I guess I survived,” I croak. I feel like I’ve been hit by a truck, which then stopped and backed over me for good measure.

But I’m not going to get any better lying on the floor, so I get up, bit by bit, testing body parts to make sure they’re all still attached. I’m remarkably intact, considering everything. The ribs are bruised, not cracked, and nothing’s broken. Win.

A long hot shower and a t-shirt and fresh pair of jeans later, I’m rustling up a good breakfast of bacon, eggs, and hashbrowns. I sit down with a loaded plate, and Tripod rests his chin on my knee and looks up at me without moving his head. I laugh and offer him a piece of bacon, and he takes it politely and crunches it down.

“Well, boy,” I say, with my mouth full of potatoes. “Petersson won’t be out until night, according to what I know about him. So maybe I should just go in and whack his head off while he’s sleeping, and then set him on *fire*. What do you think?”

His tail thumps. The concept of a “fair fight” is ludicrous, under the circumstances. Petersson is a supernatural undead creature who can turn into smoke and all kinds of other things, and I’m just a human. A United States Marine, yes, but still just human at the end of the day, and I’ll take any advantage I can get. Kill the other guy before he kills you, from behind and in the dark, if possible, because any outcome where you’re alive and the bloodthirsty monster is dead is a good one.

"It's a good day to die," said no one, ever, not really, so I amend it. "It's a good day to kill." Petersson's not human, hasn't been for a long time, and my newly-sharpened sword will separate his head from his shoulders quite adequately. I finish breakfast, put the dishes in the dishwasher, and weapon up. Tripod tries to follow me out, but I stop him. "No, you stay, boy. You don't need this." I give him a good ear-scratch before I head out, though, and tell him I love him, and that he's a good dog. With no idea how this will end, I send a brief prayer Heavenward to a God I'm not sure is listening. But I'll take all the help I can get.

The cemetery is quiet. No fog, no ghosts, no screaming. The day carries no evil portents; the sun shines, the birds sing, and it's blessedly, blessedly *normal*. I've got my sword in my right hand and the shotgun in my left, finger on the trigger because the hell with gun safety in this situation. I shoot expert with both hands, but swordplay is a different proposition. There's gasoline and a match in the garage for afterward.

Even Petersson's mound is silent. I creep into it through that awful opening and find him asleep on the king-sized bed, hands crossed on his chest. Breathing. That's wrong, that he should breathe, and I raise my sword with a snarl.

His eyes snap open just as I bring it down.

He rolls off the bed away from me, growling. The sword cleaves the pillow instead of his throat. Feathers fly everywhere. "You *dare*?" he shouts.

"Oh, you bet your ass I dare." I barely let the pillow

stop me, following through and following *him* as he leaps at me, dissolving into smoke.

But smoke I can still see, and I chase it, waiting for him to get solid again so I can make another effort at taking his head off. Sure enough, he can't actually hurt me while he's all smoky. The broken-backed horse materializes, squealing, and I swing the sword, missing the neck but connecting with the shoulder with a stroke that nearly makes me drop the blade. It feels like I whammed a rock, he's that hard.

I swallow past a dry throat. He's not even marked; my sword didn't so much as nick him. The shotgun had been ineffective last time I'd tried to use it, but my finger tightens almost automatically on the trigger. I should've worn earplugs.

The blast takes Petersson in the face, and it actually rocks him back before he drives in again. I try to dodge, but he's big and there's no room to maneuver. He slams into me, knocking me to the floor. I roll out of the way, and his hooves come down a hairsbreadth from my head, actually grazing my ear. The faded sigils on my arms and legs flare to life with dull heat. I keep moving, somersaulting toward the opening, and he keeps following, transforming into the cat as he does and swiping his claws at my legs.

I pull them out of the way, but he catches my calf anyway, leaving long bleeding scratches that burn and freeze at the same time. I aim a kick at his face, and it's like kicking a wall but actually shoves me backward in the direction of the opening. So I do it again, and he squalls as blood spurts from his nose and the sigils on that leg burn hotter.

It's the first and only time I've actually hurt him, and I'll analyze that if I ever get out of here. Another push and roll and I pop out into daylight, Petersson's roar following me out and fading away to nothing as I lie there panting.

I drop my head down onto the ground and close my eyes. Somewhere in the melee I lost the shotgun, but I'm still gripping my sword. It's a wonder I didn't stab myself with it. "Ow."

"Well, sugar, that didn't go too well." I crack an eyelid open to see Laurel standing there. Her brow creases. "You're bleeding."

"Yep." I huff out a breath, pressing a hand to my sore ribs. "How are you supposed to behead him if the sword bounces off his hide?"

"No idea. But if—" She tilts her head at my calf. The pants leg is shredded from the knee down, exposing a good bit of skin. "Isn't that interesting."

"What?" I hike up onto my elbows and take a look, but whatever it is she sees, I'm missing.

"Lookit the claw marks." She gestures. "They don't touch the sigils."

I gingerly wipe away the blood, and sure enough, the scratches go over, not through, the faded runes on my knee and ankle. "Huh. I wonder. . ." Thinking it through. "It can't get through the fence. It didn't hurt me nearly as much as it should have, and I've got these things printed on my arms and legs. I kicked it in the face and gave it a nosebleed." I push myself the rest of the way to a sitting position.

"So, if I etch the runes into my sword. Like I etched

them in the fenceposts. Do you think that would work?"

"I think it's worth a try. But I also think you should redo the ones already on your body, and add more. They seem to protect you."

I nod. That's a good plan with many excellent features. I can think of a few other things I can etch runes into as well, like bullets. Maybe my aluminum baseball bat. Overkill? Ha, no. I'm a Marine. Applying judicious violence to deadly problems is what I do.

Probably should get a move on. I don't want to tackle Petersson at night, when he's fully awake. Back to the house I go. First things first—I get my leg cleaned up and slather antibiotic ointment all over it, then wrap a bandage around the whole mess and put on a clean pair of jeans. It could probably use stitches, honestly, but I am not going into town. Not yet. This will have to do, at least for now.

I'm soon set up with the etcher, my sword, and a box of bullets. I'm careful about the runes, and I try to at least make the sword look good. After I load my Ruger and stick a spare mag in my pocket, I go to work with the marker. Arms, legs, torso, throat—I use the mirror for that, and isn't that a fun operation. I think about it for a few seconds and do my boots too. Maybe I can more than bloody its nose.

I stalk out my back door to the cemetery, sword in my right hand and Ruger in my left. The sun will go down in about an hour; I hope like hell this is over by then. One way or another.

Laurel meets me by the fence, and looks me up and

down, nodding approvingly as I jump into the cemetery. "You'll do, Joe."

"I hope so." I frown a little. "You're sure he can't hurt you?"

"He never has, I don't know why he'd start now."

"All the same, try to stay out of the line of fire, please?" The last thing I need is to worry about bystanders, especially a bystander I've come to care about, in a curious way.

"Will do, sugar. You be careful, and come back out in one piece."

I have the disquieting thought that if I die, I'll be stuck in here with Petersson, who probably won't be real happy with me. Better not die, then. "Oo-rah." I jerk my chin and stride to the mound, which is silent and still. Maybe Petersson is asleep again. I duck inside, and sure enough, he's lying on his back on the bed, hands crossed over his chest like before, with a miasma of rot filling the room. I raise the Ruger and fire at his forehead just as his eyes open.

Shit, he's fast, and the bullet only grazes him, but it at least draws blood, which is heartening. He roars and rushes me, changing forms as he does to the skinless bull. That only gives me a bigger target, and I pull the trigger again and again and again, each round striking and doing damage, I can *see* it doing damage, but he won't go down, and then I have to dodge aside before he slams into me.

He hooks with a great sweeping horn, nearly thwacking my arm. I don't have a lot of maneuvering room, and then the slide locks back on the empty chamber as I fire my last round. He staggers and sweeps his head at me again, and all I have time to do is thumb the mag release before the blunt side of a horn smacks me in the right shoulder and sends me reeling. I nearly lose my grip on the sword, but I tighten my hand just in time and bring it around, slicing at his face.

He roars again as I catch him across the eye, and he rears up, body filling the room. He'll crush me if I don't move, but there's no space to go back. Instead I do something monumentally stupid and go toward him, ducking under his belly and laying it open with my blade. He comes down and wheels, changing to the cat as he does, snarling and spitting, claws foremost.

However, I've done a good job with the runes. The claws leave bloody tracks across my stomach, but it's surface damage only. I grit my teeth, because it still hurts, and bring the sword back around, doing my damnedest to take his head off. I miss his neck as he ducks, squalling, but I catch his ear, and a piece of it goes sailing out into the room. "Why won't you just *die*?" I pant.

"Why won't you?" he growls back, and who knew he could talk in cat form?

Whatever, like I care, but he's on the defensive now and I pursue him, waving my sword in his face as he gives ground. He ends up crouched in the corner between the bed and the wall, and I raise my blade—

He braces his back legs against the wall and explodes forward, slamming me to the floor on my back. He lands on my chest, knocking my wind out, and I lay there, gasping for air that won't come.

And he gets heavier. And heavier. And heavier. My ribs creak under his weight, and he leans forward into my face, sucking the breath from my lungs.

This is how the antique store lady died. My vision goes staticky and dark around the edges, and I can't, I can't go out this way, not trapped underground like this, but there's no air, and my eyes close as my left hand relaxes and drops the gun. He hisses, fat with triumph, as something snaps in my chest.

The antique store lady didn't have a sword. With the last remaining bit of my fading strength, I bring it up and around. He's not expecting that, he thinks he's won, right up until his head separates from his shoulders and rolls across the floor while his body falls the other way.

Oxygen whooshes into my lungs. He howls, a horrible haunting sound I'll probably hear in my nightmares for the rest of forever, but it's the last scream of a dying monster, and it fades off and away with a moan and a gurgle into blessed, blessed silence. The body goes back to human, shriveled and decaying. Dead.

I let go of the sword and press my hand to my abused chest, curling over onto my side and just luxuriating in breathing for a few minutes.

A soft, hesitant voice from outside. "Joe? Are you there, sugar?"

My own voice comes out in a hoarse croak. "Yeah. I'm alive. He's not."

Laurel's relief is palpable. "Well, that's pretty spiffy, I reckon."

"Any landing you walk away from." Speaking of walking, I wonder if I'll be able to. "Gimme a minute."

"Take your time, honey. No rush now that he's dead."

I still need to light him on fire, which I have issues about, and dispose of the ashes in water. I moan and push myself to my feet, gathering the Ruger and the spent magazine as I go, stuffing them in my pocket, and staggering outside. Laurel paces up and back, up and back, swapping her opened parasol from shoulder to shoulder as she does. When she sees me, she flits over and looks at me anxiously. "You're bleeding again."

"Minor scratches. We were right about the runes. I'd be dead if they hadn't protected me."

"And the critter?"

"Headless. Good workmanship in this sword." I run my hand along the flat of the blade. "And I hope I never have to use it ever again."

Tripod cavorts up to me as I open the back door, sniffing the scratches on my stomach and whining. "Be okay, fella. That problem, at least, is solved."

And it is. I build a pit so the flames are at least contained and arrange the body inside, covered with wood and charcoal. After a long moment of hesitation, I sprinkle gasoline on top and set it ablaze. I *need* to watch the body burn down, although cold shudders clutch at me and my lungs don't want to work. Two in, hold for three, two out. Laurel puts a sympathetic hand on my back, and Tripod is a bulwark beside me.

Through the panic percolating in my chest as I keep an eye on the fire, I realize that I can do this. I'm under no illusions that slaying an outer monster has laid my inner ones completely to rest, and I've still got a long way to go before I'm completely whole again. But it's a single step along that road to recovery, and I feel a vast sense of relief that I was able to accomplish it.

After the body is reduced to ashes—surprisingly quickly—I gather them into a plastic garbage bag. In the morning, I'll rent a boat at the lake and dump them.

"So, I take it you're sticking around, Joe?" Laurel asks.

I huff out a laugh. My ribs twinge. "After a fight like that? You bet your ass I'm staying. This is my *home*."

Her lips curl upward in a slow smile. "Good. Be nice to have someone living in the place again."

And it's nice to be wanted. "Maybe I'll spruce your graveyard up a little. It's been neglected a long time."

But that's a project for tomorrow. For tonight, I'll sleep the sleep of the exhausted just with my dog curled against my chest, with no howls of the damned interrupting my rest.

Finally, my neighbors will actually be quiet.

The Deep Timber

C.R. Langille

Oh, Aspen tree, what have you seen? What do you see, when you look at me?

Utah Territory, 1884

I couldn't feel my fingers anymore, which meant starting a fire was going to be harder than shooting the ass off a fly at fifty paces. Whether or not we should even light a fire was still under some debate, as the matter of Gerald's posse and their current location was the topic on all our minds. However, freezing to death was becoming more and more likely and the option of warmth was becoming more and more desirable.

I pulled my old bearskin coat a little tighter around my body. It used to be my dad's before me, and his dad's before him. He used to tell me that Grandpa Rick killed and skinned a grizzly that attacked him up in the north with nothing but a hunting knife. Who knows if that story was true or not, but the coat kept me from dying as we rode further up the damned mountain.

The aspens gave way to pine as we climbed up in elevation. It became colder, but at least I didn't have to have all those damn aspens staring at me. The way the knots looked like eyes sent shivers up my back like they were judging me, staring at my soul or something.

I urged my horse up to the front of the line. He gave a huff but trotted through the snow.

Old Tommy was at the lead, followed by the Rotgut twins, Colt and Walter. Trailing behind us was that Navajo friend of Tommy's named Sani. I didn't think Sani was going to make it much farther. He'd taken a bullet in the leg a few days back as we made dust out of Evanston. That wound had started to sour and none of his Navajo tricks were making a difference.

Old Tommy had his hat pulled low and was smoking his pipe. He cast me an angry look as I neared.

"Think it's smart lighting that pipe of yours? I bet they can smell it over in the next canyon."

He grunted and shrugged his shoulders. "I reckon Gerald and his boys are just as cold and lost as we are up in this timber. If I'm going to freeze to death, might as well do so with a nice warm pipe full of tobacco."

Tommy wasn't wrong. We'd gotten turned around half a dozen times already. The lodgepoles made it hard to navigate and if it hadn't been for Sani, I'm sure we'd been chewing up dirt going in circles. However, Sani wasn't saying much anymore, not that the man was a chatterbox to begin with. His skin was looking mighty pale and he had that stare I'd seen plenty of times before. It was the look you'd get when Death was on your tail.

"We should probably set up camp soon."

Tommy nodded. "Sure. Let's get it done before the sun sets."

We picked a spot near the mouth of a small draw. A little creek cut through the snow and provided a bit of background noise. While it covered our sounds, it made it difficult to hear anyone coming.

Tommy strode up to me, still puffing on that pipe. I didn't like the look in his eye. His twisted mind was churning.

"Best if you take an extra blanket and go up the hill a bit, be our lookout for the night."

I took my hat off and shook some of the snow off the brim. "Send one of the Rotgut twins. Hell, they'd probably think it's some grand bandit adventure!"

Ever since Tommy brought them into the fold they'd gone on and on about living the good life, free from the law. I think they actually believed that being an outlaw meant wandering from town to town, meeting a different señorita each night, and drinking their fill of cheap whiskey. They were sorely disappointed when it meant staying on the outskirts of most places so as to not get noticed and trying not to get sick from dirty water.

"I need someone with their wits about them tonight. Sani's about to keel over and those two morons have already started into the spirits."

The Rotgut twins were singing a song about some scantily dressed whore or something and giggling up a storm. I let out a sigh as it was going to be a cold night.

"Now if you see something, sneak on back and let us know. If you can't get back in time…"

I held up a hand to stop him. "I know, I know, shoot once in the air."

"Good man. Now head on up there. I'll try and spell you in a while."

While it was kind of him to say, it was a lie. Tommy would be snoring before too long and I would on my own.

I made my way up the hill. It wasn't too far, but it was steep, and before too long I was huffing and puffing. The cool air burned my lungs and put a feather in the back of my throat. I didn't want to be drenched in sweat and die frozen under a pine tree, so I took a moment to rest about halfway up. The Rotgut's song floated up from below and I shook my head. Those bastards would be the death of us if they didn't keep it down. Hopefully, Tommy was right, and Gerald's gang was just as lost as we were. But my granddaddy always said hope was fool's gold, nice but worthless.

I was about to start my ascent again when the snap of a tree from above echoed through the draw.

I ducked down and drew my pistol.

It was loud enough it even got the Rotgut twins' attention and their song trailed off with the wind.

I glanced back down to camp. Tommy and the others were all staring up at me, their weapons drawn. After a moment Tommy shooed me onward with a wave of his hand.

I crawled up the hillside slow and easy. I didn't want to be gasping or coughing like a lunger when I got to the top. I needed my wits about me and my aim to be true. I was almost at the crest when another branch snapped, this time closer.

I stopped and listened

My heartbeat drummed in my ears, accompanied by heavy breaths. I couldn't keep the slight shake from my hand as I took those final few steps, unsure of what lay in wait for me up above. My brain tried to say it was nothing. Just old branches givin' up the fight against the weight of the snow. Hell, I'd even take Gerald and his posse. Yet my gut screamed at me, saying it was something worse than hired guns or weather-laden sticks. My gut told me to run and never stop until these damned mountains were long behind me.

I inched my way to the top and peeked over.

There was nobody there. Just trees and more snow. A couple of ravens sat on a branch of a tall pine and stared at me like I was some fool sent for their amusement. Perhaps I was.

I walked around where I thought the sound may have come from and found the source.

A dead pine had fallen over. A widowmaker.

After a moment I walked back to the edge and waved to Tommy and the gang. The Rotgut twins started singing and laughing like nothing had ever happened. Tommy nodded and emptied his pipe into the snow. Sani stared up at me with wide eyes. Even from the distance, I could see the fear.

I set myself up in a spot far away from the fallen tree.

It was stupid, but I didn't want to be anywhere near that thing when the sun decided to set. I bundled up with my blankets, but as soon as I stopped moving, the chill set in. I debated whether or not I should light a fire. It would give away my position, but on the other hand, I wouldn't be any good as a lookout if I died from the cold.

The dead see things. They can see you.

I didn't know where those words had come from. I hadn't heard anything like that before. It had come from nowhere, the idea forming in my head and burrowing deep. Perhaps I overheard Sani talking beside a campfire one night. That had to be it. He was always rambling about spiritual nonsense when he thought nobody was listening.

I rubbed my forehead. A small ache had started just behind my eye. I took a drink from my waterskin. The water was cold just like everything else, but it soothed my parched throat. The waterskin was almost empty and I'd have to remember to fill it in the morning before we broke camp and left.

Getting the fire going took some time, but it was worth it. The warmth from the flames brought my fingers back from the brink and staved off the chill enough to keep me alive.

The Rotgut twins started singing louder. Their voices rode the wind and swept past my ears with a slight warble. Generally, in tune, it was easy to mistake the singing of the Rotgut Twins as just one person; however, this song was disjointed, broken. Tommy must have got after the two, because the singing stopped just as quick as it had come, leaving nothing but silence in its wake.

Even with the biting cold nipping at my nose and seeping into my legs, it was hard to keep my eyes open. Being on the run for the past couple of days had drained me. I kept the fire going, but the rhythmic dance of the flames was beckoning me beyond the Wall of the Sleep. At one point I nodded off only to jolt awake moments later.

The crunch of a boot in the snow did the trick. I scrambled to my feet and drew my pistol.

"Who's there?"

I pulled the hammer back and pointed it into the darkness.

"If I had wanted to kill you, you'd be dead already."

Sani stepped from the shadows and into the firelight. I let out a sigh and holstered my weapon.

"Good god, don't you know it's dangerous to go slinking about?"

Sani smiled, though it was strained.

"I find it's equally as dangerous to let folks know I'm there."

I shrugged my shoulders. "Fair enough." I motioned him to the fire.

"I brought coffee."

"Well, why didn't you say so? I could hug you!"

Sani shuffled closer and sat on the ground with a groan. I dug my tin cup from my satchel and held it out so he could pour me some coffee from the pot he'd carried with him. At that moment, Sani was a godsend, an angel sent from the heavens to deliver ambrosia upon the faithful. Except, he wasn't an angel, I wasn't faithful, and the coffee, while hot, wasn't anywhere close to the food of the gods.

"How's the wound?"

"How do you think?"

I nodded. "Maybe we can get you to a doc or something in Ashley?"

"That's what I like about you, you keep ahold of hope like it is your last gold nugget."

I wasn't sure how to take that, as I had a problem holding on to money. You could ask my wife about that. One of the reasons she took the girls and went back East to her parents' house. I'm sure her parents gave her an earful about how they knew it would turn out that way and she was better off without me.

I was sure she'd take me back if I could get enough money to keep us comfortable. Old Tommy kept talking about a plan to rob the payroll and making it big. It sounded nice, but I couldn't help but wonder how my little girls were doing. Their laughs were worth more than silver or gold.

"This will all be over soon."

Sani must have seen the darkness on my face. I took a sip of coffee and let the warm liquid roll down my throat.

"I hope so. Hey, what's your deal anyway? Why are you riding with Tommy?"

Sani had been with Tommy since before I joined up. Tommy treated the man with respect and deferred to his wisdom in many situations. Once I saw Tommy knock the teeth out of a cowpoke who made an offhand remark about Sani's heritage. I didn't care much where a person was from…Navajo, Apache, Mexican, hell as long as they didn't try to kill me and pulled their weight, people were fine by me.

"I am here because of my brother."

It was Sani's turn to wear a dark mask. He lowered his head and stared at the flames of my small fire.

"I'm not following. Where's your brother?"

Sani placed the coffee pot near the fire and folded his arms into his blanket.

"He died four years ago. We were running from a posse, much like today. Only it was him who took a bullet in the stomach."

"I'm sorry."

"I told him it was foolish to follow the path of greed. Nothing good would come of it. He would not be swayed by my words, nor the words of our mother. So, I followed him. To protect him. I failed. Now I ride with Tommy because I have nowhere else to go."

I didn't know what to say, so I said nothing. A few moments later, the Rotguts started singing again. I reckon the whiskey was starting to settle in their blood and it made them anxious.

Sani closed his eyes. "We must not attract attention."

"Because of Gerald's posse?"

"Because there is something in this woods that wants us." Sani stood with a groan. "We should not have wandered from the trail. My people tell stories of foolish boys who wandered too far into the timber. The trees, they watch and wait."

He winced at his first step and wandered back down the trail. He had left me the coffee which was kind. Yet, I couldn't help but think of things other than coffee.

There was a small stain of blood in the snow where Sani had been sitting.

The Rotgut twins finally stopped their singing. Hopefully, Tommy knocked some sense into those two. About an hour later I had burned through the pot of coffee and it had started to work its dark magic on me. I got up, careful to keep my blanket around my body, although it wasn't doing much good with the biting cold. I shuffled off a few feet and answered the call of nature.

There was a crunch of feet in the snow. I turned and drew my pistol, still hanging free in the wind. It was cold but I had other things to deal with. Standing in the dark was a tall figure. The firelight hit the person's eyes just right and flashed, almost like a cougar or something. It happened so quick I couldn't focus on it.

Whoever it was had wild hair sticking out in all directions and smelled awful. Like shit and sweat. It had to be one of the Rotguts.

"What you doing up here? Did Tommy send you up?"

No answer. He just stood there and stared at me. I took a moment to do up my pants and wrap the blanket around me again.

"Well, what is it? You drunk? You can't sit up here on watch and be blasted out of your skull. Go back down there and get some rest."

Still, he stood there. I was about to walk over and push

whichever one of those damned twins it was back down the hillside when he turned and walked away. As he did, his joints made sounds like old wood groaning or the grind of bone on bone.

I went back to my fire and sat back down. I kept my gun out resting on my leg. There were more sounds coming from the darkness. Like the trees moving. Not just swaying in the wind, as the wind wasn't blowing. But like they were getting up and walking around.

I dreamt I was surrounded by old trees and they were all staring down at my corpse. They whispered things. Things I couldn't hear. Those creaks and groans of branch and bone filled the sky and soon I couldn't hear anything at all. Anything but the screams of Colt cutting up the hillside.

It was the screams that woke me.

My face flushed with heat when I realized I'd fallen asleep on watch. If Old Tommy found out, I was a dead man.

I ran over to the hillside and looked down at the camp. Colt was pacing around and running a hand through that patch of ginger mess he called hair. He was yelling about something. Something about his brother missing.

I ran down the hill and almost tripped on an exposed root. Sani was sitting on a large boulder. He had a pained expression on his face and nodded as I walked by.

"What's going on?" It was hard to get the words out. Being so high up in the mountains was taking a toll on my lungs.

Old Tommy shot me a look that sent chills up my back even in the morning cold. Colt turned my way with a crazy look in his eye. A trail of dried drool ran down his chin coupled with fresh tears that had chiseled a path down his grimy cheeks. He stumbled over to me, still drunk and grabbed my shoulders.

"You! You were on watch! What happened to him?"

I looked around and it dawned me.

"Where's Walter?"

Colt spun around in a circle and rubbed the back of his neck. His shoulder popped.

Those creaks and groans of branch and bone...

"That's what I was asking you!"

Old Tommy stepped up and put an arm around Colt's shoulder.

"It's okay. I'm sure he just wandered off in a drunken stupor. We'll find him. Hell, in this snow it will be easy to follow his tracks."

Tracks. It had to have been Walter standing outside of my campfire last night.

"Hold on, I think he came up last night. I thought he wandered back down to camp!"

I took off running back up the hill. At one point I was crawling on all fours it was so steep. My lungs burned. I should have taken my time, but if I could find the tracks perhaps I could redeem myself for falling asleep. They didn't know I passed out, but I knew and that was enough.

It wasn't the first time I'd failed at my responsibilities.

I missed my girls.

I got to the top and almost fell over as the world spun.

I sucked in big ol' gulps of air until I could finally breath then hurried over to where I camped. The pot of coffee sat next to a pile of ashes. After a quick search, I found my tracks and patch of yellow snow and it wasn't too hard to find the other tracks. I wished I hadn't though.

The tracks showed bare feet with spots of blood. Whoever made the tracks had an irregular stride, steps sometimes close together, other times longer than a normal person should have been able to step. I followed them away from my site to a patch of thick timber. Lodgepole pines stretched up into the sky like rows upon rows of jagged teeth.

The footprints stopped at the edge of the trees and disappeared. I looked all around but couldn't find them again. The hairs on the back of my neck stood up and the chirping birds went silent. Some of the trees swayed lazily with the breeze. There was a low moan of wood as a pine moved against another.

Deep in the woods, something cracked like thunder.

"Well, did you find him?"

I jumped at the voice and spun around. Old Tommy let out a chuckle and held his hands up.

"Just me."

"Good lord, Tommy! Make some noise next time."

A wave of dizziness hit me. I leaned up against one of the trees to steady myself. There was something sticky on the tree and it was warm and made me want to throw up. I pulled my hand away expecting sap, but it was some sort of black goop. I dropped to my knee and grabbed a handful of snow to wash it away. It left a black stain on my palm and made my hand tingle.

"Well?"

I looked up at Tommy. "Well, what?"

"Did you find him?"

"No, followed these tracks to the tree line," I said pointing behind me.

Tommy turned and looked.

"What tracks?"

I growled a bit and stood. "These tracks! Are you blind?"

I turned to show him but the tracks were gone. Never there.

"What in the hell?!"

Tommy placed a hand on my shoulder. He had a genuine look of concern in his eye.

"It was…nevermind. Look, I think he went in there."

In with the timber, in the with the bones, creaking and groaning, listen to the moans.

I rubbed at my forehead. "Did you hear that?"

"Hear what?"

"Nothing," I said.

"Well, if you think he went that way, then that's good enough for me. More than likely that damned fool wandered off drunk last night and is frozen to death somewhere. Take Colt and go look for him."

I shook my head. No way I was taking that crazy drunk ass fool.

"I'll go alone, it will be quicker and quieter."

Tommy's eyes went dark for a moment. "I don't think I stuttered. Take Colt. Otherwise, he'll be yelling like a madman all through these woods. Be back before midday whether you find Walter or not. We're moving then."

I sighed. I knew from experience that I wouldn't win the argument and trying to do so would only make Tommy angry. When he got angry it was like stepping into a pit of vipers, you could possibly make it out unscathed, but more than likely you were going to get bit and probably die.

"Fine. Send him up. I'm not crawling up and down that hillside anymore."

"Good boy."

Heat flashed in my cheeks. I hated it when he called me a good boy like I was a damn dog or something. I watched him walk away and contemplated putting a bullet in his back. My hand was already on my gun when I realized what I was doing. I let out a blast of breath that I'd been holding in. I couldn't figure out where that thought had come from, it wasn't like me. The world spun and I puked up coffee. It was black like the goop on the tree.

It wasn't too much longer before Colt's mumbling and bellows echoed up the hill to my ears. It was going to be a long trek through the woods. I wiped my face and waited for Colt.

We made our way through the trees. At first, Colt called out for Walter and it took me threatening to cave in his skull for him to stop.

"We'll bring down Gerald and his posse for sure if

you keep hollerin' like that!"

"We need to find Walter!"

I rubbed my forehead. A giant pain was brewing, and I wanted to get somewhere warm and sleep for a week. Instead, I was stuck in the timber with this idiot.

"We'll find him, but we need to do it quieter, or else it won't matter if we find him or not."

Colt looked at me with crazy eyes. "It don't matter if we die. We need to find him."

I couldn't respond to that kind of crazy. There wasn't anything anyone could say. So I stayed quiet.

As long as I kept moving, I stayed warm enough. I kept that wool blanket wrapped around me, but whenever we'd stop to rest or to listen, that biting cold slithered into my bones. It was during one of those stops that the cawing of crows broke through the silence. It was more than just chattering birds or warning caws, they were announcing a feast.

Something was dead.

"Come on," I said.

We made our way through the trees, but they grew closer and closer together and there was a lot of deadfall on the ground. I felt like I wasn't supposed to go any further, but I wasn't about to let some fallen trees tell me what to do. I always did what I wanted.

That's why we can't stay with you anymore. I'm taking the girls.

I shook my head to clear the voices and pressed forward. The trees tried like hell to keep us out, but we had cold determination on our side. We scrambled across a large dead pine and broke through to a clearing. It wasn't very large, hell, I could have probably thrown a tomahawk from one tree line to the other, and I wasn't even that good at it. But it wasn't the open meadow that held my attention, no, it was the blood in the snow.

There was tons of it, spread all over hell and back. And the smell, dear lord, the smell was thick with the iron-like scent of blood. It had to be Gerald's posse. There was a campfire, still smoking with bedrolls strewn about. Whatever happened, happened while they slept.

I drew my pistol and moved to get a closer look. Colt followed close behind, his gun in hand as well.

"What the hell happened here?" Colt asked.

"I don't know. Where is everyone?"

With all the blood, there had to be a body somewhere. I searched around, poking my head into a lone tent that had been set up near the trees. The side was ripped. Inside, the smell of death and shit hit me like a punch to the gut and I about threw up.

There wasn't a body, but there was a pile of entrails in the corner.

I staggered out, coughing and covering my face.

"Don't," I said as Colt wandered over to the tent. "You don't need to see that."

He glared at me and went on ahead like a stubborn mule. A second later he fell out of the tent with a wail.

"Jesus! Jesus damned Christ! What is this?"

"I don't know. Come on though, that fire was going not too long ago, let's see if we can find where they went."

I walked around looking for tracks. With the snow it wasn't hard to find them. It looked like they had run off through the woods.

I motioned for Colt and set off after them. Not sure why really. It wasn't like it would do us any good if we found the posse. Yet, there was something deep down inside that needed to know. Besides, they could have had Walter.

At the edge of the meadow, we found more tracks, different than the others. They were also barefoot, but there were a lot of them, at least a dozen sets. They circled the meadow, sticking to the tree line and had that odd gait similar to the tracks where I had set up watch. We found their horses. They were all dead, lined up and missing their heads.

Their heads hadn't been cut off, something had ripped them off. Jagged bits of flesh and bone littered the ground. This time I did throw up.

Colt stared at the horses with a wide-eyed look of someone who had lost their last ounce of sanity. A bit of drool ran down from the corner of his mouth and his hands were shaking.

"Come on, let's go," I said.

Colt didn't respond, so I just grabbed his arm and pulled him with me. We needed to find his brother and get back to camp before Old Tommy decided we weren't worth the trouble to stick around anymore.

We followed the posse's tracks further into the woods.

Whatever got them moving had lit a fire under their feet, for Gerald's boys had run from camp and hadn't stopped.

Colt followed along staring off at nothing. I'd seen that look before. Some of the men who had fought in the war had that same look sometimes.

There was a loud crack and boom as if a tree had fallen nearby. Then another. And another! It was getting closer.

I did what any sane man would have, I ran. Thankfully, Colt followed close behind. I ran as fast as I could and had to dodge trees and rocks with almost every step.

The thing followed, crashing through the forest like a stampede of angry bison. I didn't look back. I couldn't. To do so would have broken me, for if I saw whatever it was that came for us, I knew I'd be a goner.

I shouldered through some pines and found myself face-to-face with a rock wall. A breath later, Colt stumbled beside me. We were both gasping for air, sweat pouring down our faces. If the thing didn't kill us, the cold air would.

"What now?" Colt asked.

I pointed up and holstered my pistol. "We climb."

The thing was getting closer, but I scrambled up the rock wall and somehow didn't slip and fall to my death. I could picture it in my mind's eye, falling and snapping my legs, laying there in the snow as the thing slowly devoured me.

Those creaks and groans of branch and bone...

Somehow, I made it to the top and instantly wished I hadn't.

Sitting in the snow, were the horses' heads. Right next

to them, were the heads of Gerald and his posse. Their eyes had been ripped out along with the skin around their mouth, giving them all horrible grins that would have sent shivers up Death's spine.

Colt made it up right after me. He stopped before he crawled up all the way and stared at all the heads. Tears ran down his cheeks and he kept mumbling something. I couldn't quite hear what it was but did catch a word or two.

"…the eyes in the aspens…"

"What did you say?"

He stopped speaking and looked at me.

"Tell Old Tommy I'm sorry."

Before I could say anything else he let go and fell off the rock wall. He fell to the earth with a sick thud and a crack.

"No! God damn it!"

Colt looked up at me with blood coming from his nose and mouth. He opened his mouth to say something but only let out a wet gurgle. He coughed, sending flecks of bloody spittle flying in all directions.

Before I could even start to crawl back down, something grabbed him by the shoulder and dragged him into the trees. My heart froze and my stomach dropped. There was a crack…

Those creaks and groans of branch and bone...

…and then a tear. A moment later, Colt's head came rolling out into the clearing.

I ran.

I'm not sure how I found my way back to camp, or

how I didn't freeze to death, but when I arrived, I couldn't feel my hands or feet anymore. Sani was by a campfire that was burning tall and hot. I stumbled over towards it and fell at his feet. I don't know what happened next, as everything went black.

When I woke, I was back home lying in my old, rickety bed I had fashioned from a cedar. One good shake and the thing was going to fall apart. I kept meaning to fix it, or make a new one, a better one, but never got around to it. I was covered in sweat and felt hot, so I kicked off the blankets. The cool air touched my skin and I lay in the bed staring at the old timber that held our roof up.

There were giggles from the next room followed by the angry whispers of my wife telling the girls to keep quiet, lest they wanted to wake me. I smiled, couldn't help it.

I sat up and shuffled over to the doorway. My hips and shoulders hurt something fierce and my head felt like it was going to bust open at any moment. I had to steady myself before I fell over.

"Oh look, you woke up your father. He's going to be mighty angry with you."

I walked over to the table and sat in the chair. "It's okay, honey, I was already awake."

The girls giggled again and ran over to me. They were like two little angels with hair the color of a wheat field and eyes bluer than a cornflower. I scooped them up into a big hug and held them tight. They groaned and tried to get away, but I didn't want to let them go. I took in a deep breath and my heart skipped a beat.

They smelled like dead leaves and rotting meat.

I dropped them to the ground and they snapped like dried twigs. They continued to giggle. My wife ambled up behind me, lumbering like some great beast.

"He's going to be mighty angry with you."

Her voice was dry and raspy. She placed a hand on my shoulder and it was rough and skeletal.

I didn't want to turn around, but she placed another hand on the other shoulder and spun me around with profound strength.

I screamed and screamed until my throat was raw. I screamed until someone shook me so hard my teeth rattled.

"Wake up. It is a dream."

It was Sani's voice. I was next to the fire wrapped in three blankets. I scrambled backward and shed the blankets like a snakeskin.

"Where am I? What's going on?"

Sani placed another log on the fire and looked at me. His eyes were bloodshot and his skin was almost as white as the snow.

"You are back at camp."

I looked around, there wasn't anyone else. I remembered Walter had run off and Colt had…Colt was gone.

"Old Tommy?"

Sani shook his head. "Left before mid-day."

"Damn it."

"He said he was not going to die out here waiting for

you to get back."

It sounded like Tommy. "Why didn't you go with him?"

Sani looked at me and gave me a pained smile. "I'm already dead. I'm waiting for my spirit to realize it."

"Nonsense let's get the hell out of here. I have no idea where Walter went, but Colt's dead. So is the posse."

"I'm not going anywhere."

Well, I sure as shit wasn't going to stick around and freeze to death. I got up and shuffled over to my horse. At least Tommy had the decency to leave it behind, though I surmised it was more for speed than doing me any favors.

I got into the saddle and my back screamed at me to stop. I needed a bottle of whiskey and a week's worth of sleep. I looked over to Sani and found him staring back at me.

"What's out there?" I asked.

"Our sins coming for us. We are bad men. Our days of robbing and fighting could not last forever."

"That doesn't make a lick of sense," I said.

"It doesn't have to."

I wanted to be with my family. Not up here freezing to death. I gave a nod to Sani who nodded back.

It was going to be the last time I ever saw him, I knew that much. With that, I kicked my horse and headed down the trail. I needed to get off this cursed mountain and into a warm saloon soon, or I was going to be as dead as everyone else.

Old Tommy's tracks were easy to follow in the snow. It wasn't the usual route to Ashley, but perhaps he was still trying to avoid the posse. Tommy had no idea that the posse wasn't a threat anymore. I didn't want to be alone, so I kicked my horse into a run and hoped I could catch up.

His tracks wound up a hillside and back down again. A large pond that was starting to ice over came into view. Way on the other side two figures stepped out from the trees. One waved at me with jerky movements. The other didn't have a head.

It was the Rotgut twins.

I looked away and went faster. I didn't look back, afraid of what I might see, but the weight of the forest watching me was heavier than a wet wool blanket. The wind rushed past my ears and bit the skin on my face, but I didn't dare slow down. If I did, they would catch me.

"Dadda?"

The voice came out of nowhere and my horse whinnied and reared back, dumping me into the snow. Before I could get up and grab the reins it took off screaming and wide-eyed.

"Damn it! Get back here!"

It was hopeless though, that horse was halfway to Fort Bridger by now. I sat there in the snow, not sure what to do next.

There was a snap of a branch and the woods fell silent. I spun around. There, at the edge of the pines, was a group of aspen trees. Had they been there before? I didn't notice any aspens when I had ridden by, just pines.

The hair on the back of my neck stood and a shiver ran through my body. I stood and followed Tommy's trail. Thankfully it led away from those trees, as the eye-like knots watched my every movement, hungry-as if I were a prize.

As I crunched through frost-encrusted snow, there was another sound. At first, I thought it was just me walking, but I would stop, and it continued. A low creak, and snap, as wood moved.

I spun around to find the aspen trees still there, but they had changed location. They were spread out. Not just in a clump together.

I picked up the pace and started to run. As I did the Rotgut Twins started singing from the timber. Their song rose into the air and wavered. It was the same song they sang the night before, but it lacked joy. Instead, it was rushed, like they were forced to sing it faster than normal. It picked up tempo and the Rotgut Twins sang louder.

I moved as fast as I could and Tommy's trail started to go down a hill. The pines gave way to more and more aspen the further down I went.

They were all watching me, and I swore I could hear them breathing, laughing, and mocking me as I went. Then came a thunderous crack that echoed through the draw and ripped through my ears. I couldn't help but let out a cry and drop to my knees. There were creaks and groans from behind me. I didn't want to look. I wanted to keep going and find Tommy. But, I couldn't help it.

All of the aspens were bent toward me, their branches pointing at me like accusing fingers. A shadow of movement caught my eye and I slowly turned my head. Standing there in the trees was Walter. His eyes were gone and the pits looked like the knots in the trees. His grin was wide, much wider than it should have been. He pointed at me and opened his mouth.

The Rotgut's song came from deep inside him as his mouth stayed open and unmoving.

Down near the aspen trees
Feel the fear, hear the screams
Down near the aspen trees
What have you seen
What do you see when you look at me
Down near the aspen trees
With those creaks and groans of branch and bone
We'll grind your bones to dust and stone

Walter turned his head until he was looking right at me. He moved his arm and pointed a finger and when he did it sounded like trees moaning in the wind. His mouth was still open but the song had stopped. What came out of his mouth next was more horrifying than anything else.

You're never here anymore. I just don't feel safe. I'm taking the girls with me and going back home.

My wife's voice floated from deep inside Walter's body and got louder and louder until it came from every direction. I covered my ears and dropped to my knees.

"This ain't real! You ain't real!"

I screamed until my voice was shredded and broken.

When I opened my eyes, there were aspens all around me, staring at me with their black and dead eyes.

I came to, walking down the trail. I don't know how long I had been walking, but the sun was setting. I was shivering something fierce and couldn't feel my feet anymore. My legs were stiff. I wanted to tear my boots off and look, but I was afraid of what I'd find.

I was afraid they would be wood.

I stumbled down the path, catching glimpses of things moving in the trees; eyes that caught the setting sunlight just right and glowed; a clawed hand caressing a tree trunk. And the whispers, dear god the whispers. They came from the timber and told me things I never wanted to hear. Things I dare not repeat.

The trail became steep and I slipped in the snow. I hit a rock with my hip on the way down and cried out as fire burned down my leg and up my back. I rolled to the bottom and just lay there for a moment wishing I was dead.

The dead see things. They can see you.

There was another sound nearby, the crack and pop of a fire and the huff and shuffle of a horse. The pleasant aroma of coffee wafted into my nose and for a moment I thought perhaps I *had* died and this was heaven. But the pain in my back and the cold seeping into my body argued otherwise.

Besides, I had a feeling I wasn't destined for heaven.

I rolled to my stomach and pushed myself up to my knees. When I stood the pain in my hip came alive like someone had poked me with a branding iron. I wobbled to a tree and leaned against it for support.

It moved when I touched it, slithered like a bark-covered snake.

I hobbled to the fire. Old Tommy sat next to it warming up his hands.

"You made it. I always knew you would."

"What the hell is going on?" I asked.

Old Tommy poured a cup of coffee and handed it to me. I took it and just held my hands around the cup for warmth. My fingers were red and blistered.

"Seems like we've gotten trapped here. Whatever lives in these woods doesn't want us to leave. I tried every trail I knew, but kept ending up here," he said.

"But why? Why is it happening?"

Old Tommy sighed and poured himself a cup of coffee.

"My grandpappy used to tell me stories of the deep timber. How, if you went waltzin' in them woods and brought a sour heart, that sometimes it would attract the attention of them trees and those dark things that lived in them. He said, always stay on the trails and try and keep that bitterness in the foothills, for the timber was a place a violent man could meet a violent end."

He took his pipe out and lit it, and when the match flared to life, the firelight exposed his eyes. They were tree knots, twisted and black.

Tommy looked at me and smiled. His skin cracked around his lips and on his cheeks.

I turned to run and was surrounded by trees. They moved in on me, so thick I couldn't see through them.

I let out a yell and jumped on Tommy's horse. We

beat hell out of that meadow. The trees scratched at my face and grabbed my clothes. Their bony fingers dug into skin and burrowed as deep as they could as I raced past, but I didn't care. Blood ran freely into my eyes and I could barely see.

I never looked back and I pushed that horse until it died on that mountainside. Once it fell, I got up and ran. I ran as far as I could until up was down and left was right.

They say when I stumbled into the streets of Ashley I was covered in mud and blood and had a crazed look in my eye. They say it took four men to hold me down so the doc could fix me up.

But I don't remember any of it. All I remember is the trees. Those damned trees everywhere, looking at me.

The trees were one of the reasons why I was so nervous to go back east to find my family. There were so many trees out that way. Perhaps, once I found them, we could go somewhere where there weren't any trees.

I held the train ticket in my hand, a small thing but it was heavier than a sack of gold nuggets. Just looking at the damned thing got my heart running wild.

"Coming home," I said, barely more than a whisper.

The train rumbled toward the station spewing black smoke and screaming like a hellhound. It lumbered to a stop in front of me and for a few moments all I could do was stare at it. This damned thing would take me back to my girls and that was that. I was done running and gunning. I'd take a job cutting down trees or moving cattle, anything to keep them in my life. As soon as I could, I boarded the train and found a seat.

I let out a sigh and sank into the cushioned bench. I closed my eyes and just let everything go. The sounds of folks boarding the train and engaging in idle chatter filled my head.

But there was something else. A sound that sort of tiptoed through the rest of the noise. Like branches swaying in a breeze behind me.

My eyes shot open and I spun around in my chair. A woman wearing a blue dress recoiled in her seat and looked at me with wide, fright-filled eyes.

I searched, but couldn't find anything out of the ordinary.

"Sorry, ma'am."

She shot me an icy look and moved to another seat muttering about the train letting on certain types of people or some sort of nonsense. I faced forward and rubbed at my temples. Since my ordeal in the woods, the smallest thing set me on edge. I closed my eyes and rested my head against the window.

When I woke, the train was moving and we were somewhere in the plains. Rolling hills filled with grass filled the view as far as the eye could see. The wind blew and the grass gave its best impression of the ocean. Best of all, there were no trees.

My neck ached from sleeping in an odd position for too long. It was stiff and cracked when I moved it. I rubbed at the back of my neck with my hand and stopped when my fingers brushed across something hard. It was like a scab, but harder.

I picked at it and pain jumped through my whole body. Pain or not, I was damned curious now. I gritted my teeth and grabbed on to a bit of the hard substance and pulled.

Fire ran down my neck and my stomach lurched. I let out a grunt of pain but pulled some more. Whatever it was, was attached and pulled my skin along with it, tearing a bit and I yanked harder. With one final pull, it tore free, taking a strip of flesh along as a prize.

My hands were shaking as I brought the hard piece around to take a look. Sweat poured down my face and my breathing was haggard. I held a bloody strip of skin in my fingers. I flipped it over and immediately threw it on the floor.

It was a piece of bark.

Someone started humming a tune behind me, the same tune the Rotguts had sung back in the timber. I whirled and searched the faces of the passengers looking for Colt or Walter. There he was. He sat at the very back with his hat brim pulled so low it hid his face. But nothing could hide that mess of hair that was redder than a young boy's face visiting a brothel for the first time.

I stood and drew my pistol. The nearby passengers gasped and shrank away from me like I was a monster. There were screams and guffaws as I passed by. One cowpoke stood up thinking he was going to be a hero or something.

"Now put that gun away like a good boy before anyone gets hurt."

I turned my attention to the man and sneered. "This ain't any of your business, now get out of the way!"

"Want to think twice about that?" He pulled his jacket to the side and exposed a tin star on his vest. His other hand rested on the ivory-handled grip of his pistol holstered on his hip.

My mind raced. I couldn't' afford to make a scene, not when I was so close to getting back to my family. But on the other hand, *he* was back there waiting. I glanced at the back of the train, but the man was gone. I looked everywhere but couldn't find him.

"Okay, okay. Sorry about that. Just had a bit to drink and a bad dream."

I put my pistol away and put my hands in the air.

"You just sit down, be quiet and don't make any more fuss and we'll forget this ever happened. Got it?"

I wanted to bash the lawman's skull in and crack his bones like twigs.

I rubbed at my head.

"Of course, Marshal. Of course."

I went and sat back in my seat. A few of the nearby passengers got up and moved away from me. Couldn't blame them one bit.

The rest of the train ride passed without event. I spent most of the time trying to sleep and avoid the marshal. I kept an eye out for the red-haired stranger, but I couldn't find him again.

After a long journey, the train finally stopped at my destination. I stepped off onto the platform and took a deep breath. The air here was different, hard to explain. I much preferred the mountains, or I should say, I used to prefer the mountains. But in those ancient peaks was where the timber grew thick. Perhaps it would be better for a change of pace and I knew it would be better with my wife and girls.

The Marshal walked off the train and shot me a look.

He'd been eyeing me the whole train ride and I figured he might have half an idea on who I was. I was wanted in a couple of the territories.

He started to walk towards me. I pulled my hat low and walked away from him and into the biggest crowd I could find. I pushed through the people and slipped into a nearby alley. The alley smelled of piss and the muffled, off-key tune, from a saloon piano came through a nearby wall.

The sun crept through the buildings in such a way that the Marshal's shadow splayed across one of the buildings. It grew bigger as he neared. I ducked behind a stack of boxes and drew my gun. I didn't want to kill the man, but I didn't go through hell and come all this way just to end up in jail.

The shadow stopped as the Marshal rounded the corner. I wanted to peak over the boxes and see if it really was him or just some passerby, but I didn't want to give away my position.

He started to come closer, moving slowly. I pulled the hammer back on my gun and winced as it clicked into the place, sure the Marshal heard it.

He moved even closer. When stepped, his joints creaked.

Those creaks and groans of branch and bone...

That humming started again. The same humming from the train.

The shadow started to run towards me. It moved in a jerky motion like it was a scarecrow that had come to life.

The creaks and cracks got louder as it closed the distance. I scrambled backward but couldn't quite get any traction in the dirt.

Just as it was almost upon me it stopped. The boxes obscured most of it from view, but the top of its hat let me know it was standing there. Then, it spoke.

"With those creaks and groans of branch and bone, we'll grind your bones to dust and stone."

Its voice…it was deep and didn't sound like anything a human being should have sounded like. It was like the woods moving and the bugs buzzing. It was like a mountain lion screaming. It was the wind ripping the flesh from bone.

A strong gust of wind blew through the ally. It kicked up dust that got in my eyes and I had to snap them shut or go blind. I threw my hand up to protect my face, but just as fast as the gust had come, it was gone. I wiped my eyes clear and the man was gone.

I stood and pointed my gun down the alley. My hand was shaking so bad I was afraid I was going to send a round through the saloon wall on accident. I couldn't find the stranger. The only thing left was a few aspen leaves sitting in a pile behind the boxes.

I found my way to the house easily enough. Her father ran a sawmill and had made a name for himself. He owned a large estate outside of town. I walked up the steps to the front door and hesitated before I knocked.

I caught a glimpse of myself in the window and lamented my current state. My eyes were bloodshot and sunken with exhaustion. I was covered in dirt and dust and there were tears in my shirt from when…

I didn't want to think about it. I found my grit and knocked on the door. A moment later it opened, and I found myself face-to-face with her father.

He was a tall man, thin to the point of being skeletal. He sported a bushy mustache that hung off his face and below his chin that was the color ash. His eyes narrowed when he saw me.

He opened his mouth, about to spit some curses my way I was sure. I put my hand up to stop him.

"I don't want to fight. I came back because I know I made some mistakes and I want to make amends. I just want to be with my family now. I want to see my girls."

He looked at me for a moment before spitting on the ground. He wiped his mouth with a kerchief and spun on his heel. I halfway expected him to slam the door in my face and that would be it, but he took a few steps down the hall and stopped. When he noticed that I was still standing in the doorway he motioned for me to follow him.

My heart lifted and I bounded into the house after him. He led me through the main room, past the kitchen where his staff was preparing dinner. I didn't realize how hungry I was until that wonderful scent of venison stew hit my nose. My stomach growled and I had to stop myself from grabbing a slice of cheese off the counter as we passed by. I was here to make a good impression and I'd be damned if a little thing like hunger was going to ruin it any further.

He led me to the back and opened the door.

"Well, go on then," he said. His voice was gruff.

I wasn't too sure what was going on or why he wanted me to go out into the back yard. Then I heard it—the laughter of my little girls.

I stepped out of the house and couldn't stop the tears from welling up. There they were, my two beautiful girls, running in the grass chasing a couple of butterflies. Their long blonde hair flew wild as they ran and I couldn't help but laugh. They had definitely gotten their mother's hair.

The laugh caught their attention and their eyes lit up like the sun when they saw me.

"Dada!"

I dropped to one knee and caught them as they ran into my embrace. I hugged them so tight and close and simply basked in their smell. I kissed their heads and kept hugging them.

"Daddy's home, my angels."

"For how long?"

"For good this time."

"Is that so?" My wife asked from behind me.

I let my girls go and stood to face her. She wore a grey skirt with a white top. Her hair was pulled up with a loose strand dangling in her face. Her eyes were wet with tears as well and she was trying to be stern with me, but I could tell she missed me just as much as I missed her.

I took two steps forward and picked her up off the ground and spun her in the air. She let out a little squeal and the girls giggled. I let her feet touch the ground and pulled her close and kissed her. Her lips were warm and tasted slightly of peppermint.

"It's so," I said. "I promise. No more outlawin' for me. I'm done."

She didn't say any words, but her eyes told me everything. She hugged me tightly.

The girls resumed their pursuit of the elusive butterflies. I sat on the porch and wondered why I ever left in the first place.

As I sat there, something caught my eye. Something nestled back in the hickory trees. I stood and walked towards it. It was white.

My legs began to shake as I walked. It couldn't be.

There, standing alone amongst the ancient hickory trees was a lone aspen.

My girls ran towards me and their bones creaked and groaned.

Part IV: Quests

ΔΦ ЃΤ

Short Fiction

NO SOLICITING

CARYN LARRINAGA

At twelve o'clock in the afternoon, just as it had every day for the last five weeks, the bell rang. Doris scowled at the front door from her indentation on the sagging couch and braced herself for the subsequent rings.

"Go away! Go away!" Frankie shouted from his perch.

"Frankie, quiet!" Doris hissed.

Her admonition made no difference. The parrot hadn't listened to her in twenty-five years; why on earth would he start now? And no matter how much either the bird or the woman told the salesman to leave them alone, he paid her even less heed than Frankie.

The doorbell rang again.

"Ma'am?" The salesman's voice pierced through the reinforced door. "I know you're in there. Please, I'd just like to talk to you for a few minutes about your home's security."

Doris rolled her eyes and turned her TV's volume up as far as she could stand it. She'd never stood on her front porch while the TV was on—or ever, come to think of it—but she felt confident the salesman could hear the soap opera stars shouting about the main character's sister returning from the dead. Doris grinned, imagining the salesman getting sucked into the story but never having the satisfaction of knowing how it ended. She would turn the volume down before any kind of big reveal. It'd be easy; she could always feel them coming, the way the mood of the music would shift and intensify right before the surprise came.

The faint sound of a fist pounding on the door reached her ears through the noise from the television set. The doorbell rang a third time. A minute later, the top of a blue baseball cap bobbed past the front window, away from the porch.

Joints creaking, Doris struggled off the couch and shambled to the window. The salesman, a youngster somewhere in his early twenties, stopped at the end of her long driveway and looked back at the house. She didn't bother to hide herself. He knew she was home. He knew that she knew that he knew, but it didn't stop him from harassing her day after day. Had she been so headstrong in her youth? The twin veils of time and malnutrition obscured her memory. A hundred years was far too many to reflect upon with such an empty stomach.

"Go away!" the parrot shrieked.

Doris snorted and turned away from the window. "Stupid bird. He's gone. For today, anyway."

Not bothering to turn down the television, she shuffled into the kitchen. A frying pan filled with a thin layer of oil waited on the gas stove. She retrieved her last packet of meat from the old, grumbling freezer and threw the steak into the pan. As the thigh sizzled and hissed, a jagged grin spread over her wrinkled face. Her freezer was empty. The next delivery would come tonight: fresher meat, and the extra little something she had ordered. Soon, she would have peace again.

±A±

Too excited to sleep, Doris perched on a short wooden stool by the back door, watching the second hand of the big clock over the stove ticking closer to midnight. The hour came, and she craned her neck, straining to hear the telltale sounds of her monthly delivery.

There would be no knock, no doorbell ring. The faceless, nameless courier never deviated from the routine. Every thirty days, he left sixty cutlets of fresh meat and any other requested sundries—pellets and produce for Frankie, poison for the rats in the basement, cooking oil—in the old wooden box on the back porch. Doris would confirm the delivery with a phone call, usually the next morning, and the money would get transferred from her account to the company's.

In over two decades of solitude, Doris had only needed to change this service once. A few years into their contract, the first company had gotten lazy, started cutting corners with the harvest. She'd felt the age of the meat at once; her joints had locked up and she'd lost several teeth. It'd taken all her energy to telephone the remaining brethren in her little book of contacts—even then, too many names had been crossed out—but luckily, one other of her kind smart enough to close themselves off from the world had recommended an alternate service.

The new company proved to be excellent. They sourced the meat only from the most reputable of morgues, and guaranteed harvest and flash-freezing within forty-eight hours of death. They were discreet and protected the privacy of their customers. Best of all, delivery was never late.

A low thump sounded from the porch, and Doris' black eyes lit up with excitement. It took all her willpower to wait a full five minutes, a window of time required by the delivery company for their staff's safety. At last she pulled herself to her feet, unfastened the chain, released the four deadbolts, and opened the door. With as much speed as she could manage, she ferried the packets of meat from the delivery box and into her kitchen. Beneath the last paper-wrapped package, she found the thing she'd been anticipating as much as—more than, really—the meat: a small, magnetic sign.

After re-locking the back door, she carried the sign through the house to the front door. It took several long minutes to get the heavy, steel slab open; unlike the locks at the back of the house, these hadn't been turned in too many years to count.

At last, the door opened and Doris slapped the new sign on the front with a triumphant, "Ha!" Silver letters spelling NO SOLICITING gleamed in the moonlight.

"Let him try to come now," she told Frankie.

The bird, asleep in his cage beneath a white sheet, didn't

answer. It was for the best. She wouldn't have liked what he had to say.

±Δ±

Doris broke her fast early the next day, heating the oil on her stove well before the normal hour. Wielding her butcher's knife with more energy than usual, she cut the steak into thin strips and tossed them into the pan. The aroma that wafted upward told her this meat had come from someone who'd been alive less than two days before. It was markedly more fresh than what she'd been eating the last week, and she felt its effects mere minutes after finishing her meal. The inflammation in her joints subsided, the skin on her hands smoothed out, and her mind sharpened. She stood in front of the mirror by the front door for a while, admiring the difference in her face. She didn't look a day over eighty.

"Hey, old lady!" Frankie squawked from his cage.

"Oh, shut up." She touched the corners of her eyes, where deep crow's feet betrayed too many decades of glaring at that stupid bird. She wondered what she would've looked like at sixty, fifty, or even thirty-five. With enough fresh meat, could she see?

It'd have to be quite fresh, her sister's voice purred inside her mind. *Not even dead a minute, and raw, so very raw—*

"Quiet!" Doris shouted. She glared at her reflection, seeing far too much of her sister's features in the face that glared back. But wrinkles had never softened her sister's face;

Ethel's skin had been smooth as glass when she'd gone mad.

From the box above her head, the doorbell chimed. Doris jumped, staring at the door with wide eyes.

"Ma'am?" the salesman's voice called. He knocked a few times, then rang the bell again. "Hello? We're having a sale on motion sensors and cameras. You can't put a price on your safety!"

Doris glanced at Frankie, her mouth open in hopeless shock. The salesman stood on the porch, inches away from her NO SOLICITING sign, ringing her doorbell with impunity. She backed away from the door, grateful for her fresh breakfast as she crouched on the floor beside the bird's cage, something her knees wouldn't have let her do the day before.

"What do I do?" she whispered.

"Eat him! Eat him!" Frankie suggested.

Doris smacked the bird's cage. "Don't be stupid."

"Eat him!" the bird urged again.

"You'd like that, wouldn't you?" Doris said. "You'd love to see me go insane, leave this house on a binge like your old master."

Frankie bobbed his gray head in his cage.

"What, you think someone will come rescue you? Take over your care and feeding when I'm gone, like I did after Ethel? There's nobody left who even knows we're here, you stupid creature."

The parrot held still a moment, head cocked to the side as though considering her words. Then he blinked his yellow eyes and screeched, "Old lady, old lady!"

Doris balled her hands into fists and shuddered. If any meat aside from human flesh offered her any sustenance at all, she'd eat the damn bird and be done with it. "I should leave you on the porch," she told him. "Cage and all. Let this foolish salesman take you home."

As though in answer to his title, the nuisance outside rang the bell again. After a moment, he beat on the door, pounding against the metal.

Doris shook with rage. From the height of the sound, he had to be banging his knuckles on top of the sign she'd stuck there the night before. There was no question; he saw the words, but they did nothing to deter him.

Each knock reverberated in her bones. Her teeth rattled, and she dragged her nails from her shoulders to her elbows. "Go away!" she screamed at the door. "Leave me alone!"

"Sounds like this is a bad time," the young man called. "I'll come back another day."

At that, anger took over Doris' body. She leapt to her feet, and her hand closed around the top deadbolt.

"Open!" Frankie screeched from his cage. "Open, open!"

His voice snapped Doris back to her senses. Her fingers fell away from the bolt, and she ran a shaking hand down her face. That had been far too close. In her mind's eye, she saw what had almost happened: flinging open the door and falling upon the man, ripping and tearing at his throat with her teeth like the ancient, savage monsters from whom her kind had descended. She remembered the feel of hot blood in her throat and gulped. Once, and only once, had she given in to the wild desires that lay deep within her belly. At Ethel's urging, she'd tasted the flesh of a man whose heart still beat in his chest. The memory of the sudden surge of strength and the sharpening of her mind gave Doris a fraction of the high she'd experienced that day, and she sagged against the cool metal door, heart racing and cheeks flushed.

You can feel it again, Ethel promised inside her mind. *It would be so easy.*

"No!" Doris shook her head and hugged her knees against her chest. She couldn't follow Ethel down that dark path, no matter how her sister's voice called to her. She'd seen firsthand what happened when someone gave into their bloodlust. The line between eternal youth and certain madness was thinner than Doris's ragged hair.

When her breathing slowed, she pulled herself to her feet and hobbled to the stove. Another few days of solid, unfrozen meals and her sister's voice would retreat to the corners of her mind. The fuller she was, the safer everyone would be.

± A ±

Doris woke to the sound of rain pounding on the roof, and a deep sigh escaped her lungs. Foul weather was a far more effective deterrent than a flimsy little sign. At last, a day of peace. She lay in bed a while, planning her morning. First, she'd have a fresh steak from the refrigerator, one of the last before she'd need to switch to the frozen ones. Then she'd spend the day cleaning and straightening up the house while the boost of energy lasted.

She padded into the kitchen to fry up her breakfast. In front of the fridge, the floor glinted strangely in the gray light from the window. She reached down, testing the sheen with a finger.

"Water," she murmured, furrowing her brow and glancing at the sink. The faucet was still, and she heard no signs of dripping. Where else could it have come from?

She whipped her head toward the refrigerator, registering the silence around her. The entire house was eerily quiet. Thunder cracked overhead as she flicked the light switch on and off to no effect.

The power was out.

Doris swore, and Frankie picked up the word, repeating it at top volume in the living room.

"Quiet!" she shouted.

"Quiet! Quiet!" Frankie screeched, hopping in his cage.

Ignoring the bird, she tore open the freezer's door. Half the frost inside had melted and pooled on the kitchen floor. The rest had soaked into the paper-wrapped packages she'd thrown into the compartment just two days before. She touched one; it was no longer frozen, but it smelled far from fresh. Bad or even diseased flesh wouldn't kill her, but old meat would do nothing to keep her body from racing toward its true age.

The real tragedy waited in the refrigerator. The antique appliance struggled to keep cool even with a running motor, and an unknown number of hours with no power had allowed every gasp of cold air to escape through the cracks in the door's seal. The freshest steaks, the ones she'd been counting on to wind her body's clock back to seventy or so, had turned.

She wasted no time grabbing the telephone and dialing the delivery company. "The power's gone out," she barked into the receiver when they answered. "Half my food is ruined. I need a replacement delivery."

"No problem at all," the young man on the phone replied. "We'll have that to you by midnight."

The arrangements made, Doris hung up the phone and fired up the gas stove, grateful she at least didn't need to eat her breakfast raw.

± A ±

Both the rain and the power outage continued through the next morning, but the delivery box on the back porch was empty when Doris checked it.

"We're currently experiencing a high call volume," a recorded voice explained when she called the delivery company. "Please continue to hold."

Swearing, Doris hung up the phone and checked the freezer. The situation was even worse than the day before, and she retrieved a soggy packet of meat with a disgusted groan.

Her joints ached as she prepared her breakfast at a fraction of her usual pace, not bothering to cut up the steak before searing it. She winced each time she glimpsed her hands as she ate; the blue veins beneath her paper-thin skin had never been so visible before. She'd look and feel her full hundred and six years by the day's end.

It seemed like a waste of energy to chew meat that was too old to do much more than give her the energy to chew more meat. Was this how humans felt about their food? Eating just for the sake of having enough calories to move their frail bodies around, knowing they'd continue to age and weaken with every passing day? How pointless.

But humans were lucky in some ways. She'd watched the reality TV shows about the people who were as trapped in their houses as she was in hers. At least they had visitors, family and friends who could help them pass the time. There were a handful of other unnatural beings left in her book of contacts, but none of them were any more likely to leave their hiding places than she was to leave hers, so couldn't be counted on to keep her company. And no matter how much a human ate, they'd never go mad and lose the ability to stop killing and eating before turning on their own kind.

I would never have hurt you, Ethel claimed inside her mind. *I only wanted to help you be free.*

Doris snorted and shook her head. That was another way these humans on the television were luckier than her: their siblings would never have to kill them just to stop their bloodlust from exposing their way of life.

Well at least I died young, Ethel's voice sneered. *I don't even recognize you, old woman.*

"Old woman! Old woman!" Frankie echoed from his perch.

Doris lacked the strength to argue with either of them.

She sank down onto the couch and reached for the remote before remembering there was no power. Too tired to get up, she closed her eyes and tried to nap.

DING-DONG!

The ring of the doorbell startled Doris, and she jerked forward.

"Ding-dong! Ding-dong!" Frankie helpfully sang.

Doris struggled to her feet, wondering why on earth the delivery man would ring the bell. Twelve hours late, and in broad daylight… and at her front door. She was halfway across the room before she realized he would never do such a thing. And that meant it had to be—

"Ma'am?" the salesman called through the door. "Are you home? I'd love to come in and chat with you about your home security. Do you currently have an alarm provider?"

Before she could stop them, Doris' feet carried her across the floor and into the foyer. Her hands were upon the lock, ready to pull the door open.

Yes, Ethel encouraged. *Let him come in. He's been begging for this for weeks.*

Doris examined herself in the mirror beside the door. New wrinkles lined her face, but it was Ethel's dark eyes that stared back at her.

"I couldn't," Doris told her reflection.

But you want to, Ethel said. *I can feel it. You've wanted this for twenty-five long years. Eat him. Drink his blood while it still pumps through him, and you'll be young again within the hour.*

The salesman pounded on the door. Doris rested her hand on it, inches from where his fist connected with the thick steel, and eyed her skin with distaste. Her stomach growled. She glanced helplessly at her reflection, and Ethel's eyes repeated their argument.

A memory flooded into Doris's mind. She remembered the day, so many years ago, when Ethel first convinced her to break the boundary between fresh meat and living flesh. The taste of warm blood coated her throat, and she licked her lips as her fingertips found their way to the topmost deadbolt yet again.

The door groaned as she inched it open.

"Need a hand?" the salesman asked.

"Yes, please," she said, stepping back. "It's an old door. Stubborn, like me."

The salesman laughed as he pushed his way inside the house. As Doris had guessed, he was in his early twenties, fresh-faced and tanned from day after day canvassing suburban neighborhoods. His blue cap matched his collared polo shirt, and his backpack lent an extra layer of innocence to his already youthful appearance. It'd been so many years since she'd been this close to a living human. He smelled as fresh as the rain outside.

Delicious, Ethel's voice said in chorus with her own thoughts.

He wiped his feet on the seldom-used mat inside the door, shrugging an apology for dripping water onto the hardwood.

Doris shook her head. "Please, don't worry about it. Come in. Sit down."

As the salesman walked past his cage, Frankie screeched, "Get out! Get out!"

The young man nodded to the bird. "Is it friendly?"

Frankie bobbed on his perch. "Frankie, be my friend! My friend!"

"When he wants to be," she said. "I'd keep your fingers away from the bars. He'll nip at you, and his little beak might break your skin."

The man who'd been pestering Doris for weeks slung his backpack off his shoulders and sank into Doris's spot on the couch. He took off his baseball cap, ran a hand through his thick hair, and nodded at her cluttered living room. "Lovely home. How long have you been here?"

"Oh, about twenty-five years." She smiled at him, wondering if her hair would grow back as thick and dark as his after she'd eaten his scalp. "Tea?"

"Yes, please."

He opened his backpack and began pulling out pamphlets and pricing sheets, and she left him in the bird's company. She rounded the corner into her kitchen and pulled down the teapot as quickly as she could manage, marvelling at the speed of her hands as she reached for the box of rat poison she kept in the cupboard. She moved faster than she had just an hour ago, bolstered by the anticipation of her first truly good meal since the day she'd killed Ethel.

The memory of stabbing her sister with a silver knife

stopped Doris's hands just before they closed around the poison. She'd ended Ethel's life... but why? What could make her do such a thing? Her mind clouded, and Ethel's voice tried to drown out the truth, but Doris remembered. Ethel had given in to the bloodlust. She hadn't been able to stop. And even in an era of serial killers and highway murderers, the humans had become suspicious.

I was weak, Ethel explained. *You've always been the strong one. You stopped after just one taste of a fresh kill. How many of our kind can say the same?*

It was true. Not many had the will to secrete themselves away, to allow their bodies to grow old and keep a distance from their prey. Once they'd given in to their darkest desires, the lucky ones were put down by other members of their flock. The rest got sloppy enough to attract the attention of cleverer-than-average humans and some hunter stepped in to stop their rampage. Too few had the willpower to stop killing once they'd started, to cease binging once that first juicy morsel had passed their lips.

Doris eyed the butcher's knife in the block beside the stove. Yes, that was the compromise. She'd allow herself just a taste of living flesh. A few mouthfuls, nothing more. Enough to turn back the clock a few decades, feel closer to her normal self. Then she would stop, carve up the rest of his body and store it the way her mother had taught her when she'd been a child. In the decade of plenty the humans called the "Dustbowl," her mother had dried meat into jerky, striking a perfect balance between freshness and safety. Decayed enough to keep the madness at bay, new enough to keep their family young and healthy. No freezer required.

"Sugar?" she called to the young man in her living room as she poured the poison into his cup.

"No, thank you."

With shaking hands, she carried the pair of teacups into the living room. The salesman accepted his doctored tea, smelling it with a smile before resting it on the coffee table. Doris sat down on the opposite end of the couch, her un-poisoned cup still in her hands.

"Not safe!" Frankie screeched. "Get out!"

Doris glared at the bird.

"Quite a vocabulary he has," the salesman said.

"Television," she explained. "He watches it with me, and I watch it a lot."

The young man laughed. "You and me both. Have you seen our commercials? They run pretty often."

"I haven't. You must be freezing after walking around in all this rain." She sipped her tea and nodded toward his cup. "Go on, drink up while it's hot."

Ignoring the tea, the salesman handed her a pricing sheet with text and numbers in large print. She raised a hairless eyebrow, at once grateful and irritated. Soon she'd have her full eyesight back and wouldn't need thoughtfully oversized literature.

"Have you ever had a home security system before?" he asked.

Doris shook her head. "I've never needed one."

"Could've fooled with me that big steel door." The young man grinned. "I haven't seen one of those outside a bank before. But the trick is to combine that with the newer technology we have available, like doorbell cameras and motion sensors. Times are changing. It's not safe to leave your door unlocked anymore. You never know who might turn up on your porch."

Doris wanted to laugh. Once she had her strength back, no human could defend against her if she wanted to come into their home and eat them while they slept. No camera could stop her teeth from ripping into their tender flesh—

"Not safe!" Frankie screeched again. "Run away!"

"Quiet, you stupid bird!" Doris shouted. Then she smiled an apology at the salesman. "I've got to stop letting him watch those late night horror movies after I've gone to bed. He's picking up the strangest phrases."

The salesman laughed and picked up his teacup. "They're funny little creatures, aren't they? I've always kind of wanted one."

Doris snorted. "He's all yours."

"Mmmmmm." The salesman sniffed his tea. "Smells wonderful."

He raised the cup to his lips, staring down at the liquid that would soon render him immobile. Doris wiped her mouth, which threatened to overflow with a sudden abundance of saliva.

"Look out!" Frankie screeched.

As the cup touched his lips, the salesman flicked his

eyes upward. His gaze met Doris's. Any trace of friendliness had disappeared, and she recognized the sudden hardness that took its place. It was the same glint of sharpened instinct that had filled Ethel's eyes at the end: the piercing stare of a killer.

Run! Ethel's voice screamed in her mind.

But it was too late. The hunter was upon her in an instant. She had no energy to fend off his attack, and moved too slowly to stop the descent of the blade in his hand. She screamed as it stabbed her, writhing in agony as the silver burned into her flesh.

"Bye-bye!" Frankie said.

"Damn bird," she muttered. Then, she lay still.

The hunter rose, cleaning his knife on the edge of his blue shirt. The kill had been quick and clean, the way his father had taught him. He left her valuables in place, picking up only the little leather-bound book of contacts Doris had kept by the phone. He flipped through the pages, smiling at the few names that hadn't been crossed out and recognizing some of the ones that had. Pocketing the book, he strode across the living room and picked up Frankie's cage.

"Come on, buddy," he told the bird. "You're mine now."

Frankie bobbed on his perch. He didn't mind at all.

The Wild Hunt

Cecily Kingston

To be read aloud

They are after me, the restless dead. They seek me out in the shadows and wait for me at the close of day. Flying from the west, the cruel claws of fate reach toward my soul.

My heart is blackened by this world. Some time ago, I would have been content with either life or death. I felt so trapped. Trapped in the monotony of the prison that I called life and the dreadful sameness, the agonizing routine. But then they began to circle, like ravens waiting for wolves to finish with a carcass. My mother had always been superstitious before she died, so when they came hovering around me, I recognized the signs—however much I wished I didn't. I thought I was insane at first, but apparently, I'm just as superstitious as my mother.

At that point I realized that I didn't want to die. Even this cage of precision would be better than what they had in store.

The hosts prey on the weak of heart; I suppose that was the beacon that first led them in my direction. They find the dark of mind and soul. Restless. Unburied. When they find me—the hosts—they will steal my soul. Is my purpose simply to join their battalion of the destructive and vicious, my humanity lost? Endless pain. Unstoppable darkness. Ever-present insanity. What worth would I possess as a shattered soul?

I never understood what it meant to die until they crept into the corners of my vision. Never quite in sight, but always there. A shadow of dread that settles at the back of my mind. An echo of death in my consciousness. A song of insanity. They came, the darkness with wings, and took my hope of rest in the eternities.

The hosts—after my aching soul—beckon me to join their flock.

Their wings will cut like shattered glass. They already darken my view and turn everything to shades of grey. They are the weight that lies on my shoulders and the pull at the back of my eyes. The stars don't shine as bright, and the wind has turned to ice against my skin. I can feel them in the silence, endeavoring to steal my breath away. For the first time in my life, I fear the sunset. I am dying.

Dying?

Please? No.

I don't want to die!

What pathetic lot in life is this? To be reduced to begging for my life as a feeble shell of what I could be. There must be some way for me to live. My mother mentioned them in her stories, but she never thought that I would need an escape.

When it started, it seemed so innocent: the shadows lengthened ever so slightly, and the sky grew darker. I became more desperate as the wind grew louder outside my door each night. The shades of the unforgiven dead began to chase me whenever I walked alone. I was no longer trapped by monotony, but trapped by the terror of the demons that stalked my soul. My search began—a frantic effort to save myself.

It's remarkable what you can find in a used bookstore if you're motivated enough to keep looking. It says right here, in this little green book with ripped pages and the smell of mildew: "The only escape to be made is in the form of sacrificing another."

To sentence another to that eternal torment, that anguish of soul? How could I do such a thing? To commit such an act, to be so calloused and unfeeling as to drop another unsuspecting fool into the belly of the beast, could I have fallen so far? Would this assistance to murder cease to make my stomach turn if my mind began to twist? If I fell to the self-serving creature in my head?

Misery loves company, I suppose. Even the souls of the damned.

But then. . .

I don't want to die.

Would it be worth it, knowing that I was leading them into death itself? Into the darkness of the fallen fae and restless dead? A banshee's cry would be less cruel.

And yet. . .

I don't want to die.

But I wonder, if it were a stranger, could I do it? I think so. Someone I didn't have to look in the eye. If I never had to know that they were dead, could I?

After all, I could be delusional. Nothing more than fanciful and overenthusiastic superstition. That flutter of wings, that wail of the dead, could be no more than the wind in the dark. Those savage claws could be nothing more than a branch across the window. The shattering chill that comes to me when the sun begins to set could be nothing but my mind playing tricks. Yes, that's it, I may be mad! If they left me, I would have no way of knowing. Maybe they have left me for another, but perhaps they were never really there.

But still. . .

I don't want to die.

Yet, if I wasn't mad and they came like condemning angels from hell, if they took all I have left and my soul was stolen, I would become one of them. They would take me as part of their flock and I would be as lost as they.

The darkness. The fallen. The Sluagh.

There.

It's done.

There are two ways to gain their attention, you see. The first is to be a weak or dying soul. The second, however, is far easier to orchestrate: The Sluagh will hunt all those who speak their name. You, unlucky stranger, fall into that place. I truly wish it hadn't come to this, but I'd rather it be you than me.

I pray for you, stranger, that perhaps you may escape their grasp.

It will begin with nothing more than a chill in the air as soon as the sun sets, coming from the west. The wind will swirl and shriek until you can't tell whether it is your imagination or a beast outside your door.

You'll start to see them on the brink of your subconscious, like the creature you saw in your closet when you were young—it could be nothing more than a winter coat, but it may be fangs waiting to close around your throat.

Nothing at first but a pull at your mind. Nothing but a sense of dread that grows as they draw closer. Nothing but an echo of an ache in your heart, like a piece of you is missing.

Nothing until they find you, and rip your soul from your body. And then, only then, will you feel the eternal agony that you didn't know you were dreading.

It may be, if Lady Luck is on your side, that someone reads this after you. It may be that you never encounter them in all your days of living. But it may be that your voice is the last one they hear. If so, they will be after you.

I offer some advice now, if you want to save your soul, if, indeed, you are the next name on their list. From darkness they creep, to steal the souls of the broken and the dying. For they are fallen, forever uneasy with their lot. They wish their misery upon the world and any who live within it. Avoid the darkness, for in it they thrive. Stay inside at night, for they will find you in the chill of the night air. Simple though they may be, these actions can save you for a while. But nothing lasts forever, so here, poor stranger, is my last bit of advice: Pray.

You may try to run from the Sluagh, to run from their shadows. Do what you can to escape them for as long as you can, but as running has never saved anyone before—pray for your soul. I will do the same. May they be kinder to you than they were to me.

But either way, I. . .

I will live.

Her Skin

Maegan Langer

He found her in Hells Canyon. After that, my friend Oss liked to brag about how he'd gone fishing in the Snake River and caught a wife instead, but I knew it was really the other way around.

Recently off our missions, Ossman and I were backpacking in Idaho that summer, like we had done so many summers before. The ancient rock walls of the gorge were a convenient buffer against the real world. Neither one of us knew what we wanted to do next with our lives.

That day, we were fishing for trout in one of our favorite spots, where the river cut a small hidden bend into the canyon and we could cast from the boulders right out in the water. We'd stay like that for hours, not talking, just hearing the water and the gulls overhead, waiting for the tug that signaled we'd caught a bite. Having first discovered the place as kids, we liked to think we were the only ones who knew about it. I'd caught the most so far, but Oss was catching up. He stepped away to the shore to take a leak in the trees. I didn't pay much notice, until I realized he hadn't come back.

"Oss?" I called. I didn't see him anywhere, so I sloshed through the ankle-deep water back to the shore. His pack was gone too. A snap of wood behind me made me turn, and there was Oss emerging from the sagebrush with a big, dumb smile on his face. But he wasn't alone. He was leading a young woman by the hand. Water dripped from her long, black hair, ran down her elongated limbs. She reminded me instantly of a praying mantis. She wore nothing but Oss's flannel shirt, barely long enough to cover the essentials. She seemed completely unbothered by the rocks and grit beneath her bare feet. And her skin—I don't know. Is colorless a color?

"Who's this?" I asked.

"This is, um," Oss looked at the girl and back to me.

"Emily. Her name's Emily."

That was weird. Everything about this was weird. Oss seemed. . .changed. He looked so happy. It couldn't be real. Meanwhile, my lizard brain was telling me to get out, to run. There was something not right about this girl. Something *alien.* So much so that it was difficult for me to look at her.

"What are you doing out here, Emily?" She just stared at me, so I tried again. "Are you alone? Do you speak English? Hablas español?" Still nothing.

For Oss's sake, I stepped forward and held out my hand. This time, the girl looked to Oss. He only smiled bigger and dumber. She reached out her hand and took mine. Maybe it was the gathering storm clouds overhead, or maybe it was just my imagination, but in that moment, I felt a pop of static electricity leap from her clammy palm to mine.

"What's the story, Oss?" I tried to keep the suspicion out of my voice as I rubbed my tingling palm on my shirt.

"I found her in the trees. She's lost." Clearly, he wasn't about to offer any more than that.

"Then we should take her to the ranger station. Or the police."

"Sure. But first, I'm taking her home."

"What?"

"Look at her. She's got nothing. She needs clothes."

"They have supplies at the ranger station."

While we argued, she watched. I mean, really *watched,* with eyes so dark brown they were almost black. In all the time I would know her, I never once saw her blink. I noticed, though, that her expression changed from wide-eyed innocence to one of knowing whenever Oss wasn't looking at her. She may not have spoken English, but somehow she understood everything that was happening. In fact, I think she enjoyed it.

"I'm not leaving her with a bunch of strangers," Oss said.

"*We* are strangers," I pointed out. "Do you know how weird you're being right now?"

"She needs help. We can help her!"

I put my hand on Oss's shoulder to guide him a few steps away, out of her earshot. "This girl just appeared in the middle of nowhere and you want to take her home like a stray cat or something. That doesn't seem crazy to you?"

"What are you so afraid of?" Oss laughed. "You think she's gonna strangle us with my shirt?"

"What if she's a minor? We could get arrested for kidnapping."

"She's not—" Oss looked to the girl, who stood eerily still on the shore staring at us, and back to me. "She's not a minor."

"How do you know? She show you her ID?"

"Look. I drove, dude. Remember? I'm taking her home. Come with us, or hitchhike. Your choice."

He stalked away from me before I could respond, shouldering the pack he'd brought back with him out of the trees. The girl latched onto him. Without looking back, they started up the long trail leading away from the shore to the car. Just like that, this strange girl had made me excess baggage in my best friend's life.

So we brought her with us on the six-hour drive back to Salt Lake City. I sat in the back seat with the girl riding shotgun. Not only because Oss asked me to, but because it was easier to keep an eye on her that way. On both of them. The thought of her sitting behind me for any length of time was enough to make me nauseated. They held hands the whole way home. Even when Oss had to shift gears, she kept her hand on top of his.

Within a week, they were married. Oss gave his bewildered family barely enough notice to travel in from California for the wedding. I spent that time scouring local police bulletins and news stories for any signs of a missing girl or even an escaped psychiatric patient. Nothing. It was like she appeared straight from the ether. I still tried my best to talk him out of it, to wait a few months at least, but Oss was adamant.

For a while, things seemed to work well enough. She galvanized him to move forward with his life. He got a part-time job, went back to the U, and they moved into an old house with a porch and a flower bed and Red Butte Creek a stone's throw away out back. The local ward accepted Oss's new wife with almost terminal politeness. Any talk of her getting baptized, however, was oddly shut down by Oss.

It seemed like whenever I went to the house to see Oss, she was upstairs, taking a bath. We could hear her splashing through the ceiling. "I swear, she spends more time in there than she does with me," he joked.

And then, barely a year after the wedding, the baby was born. I arrived with a bouquet of flowers just as an ashen-faced midwife rushed out the front door to her car. Meanwhile, Oss waited for me on the porch, practically vibrating with happiness.

"It's a girl," he announced in a manic stage whisper. "Come and see." I followed him to the upstairs bedroom, where his wife sat swaddled in the dark in the middle of their bed, gently rocking back and forth.

She shrunk away from the light when Oss switched on a bedside lamp. Her damp hair was plastered against her forehead, snaking down her neck in long black tendrils. She clutched a bundle of gray towels close to her face, oblivious to everything else. An odd humming emanated from her throat. It was the only sound I'd ever heard her make. Oss perched himself on the edge of the mattress and beckoned me to come inside.

Stepping into that room was the last thing I wanted to do. I remembered my sister the day my nephew was born, exhausted, but radiant in her hospital bed, surrounded by bright flowers from well-wishers. This was different. The air beyond the threshold was dense and humid, with a stench equal parts rotten and metallic.

Oss was still looking at me. I entered, holding the bouquet up to my face as a shield against more than just the smell. For Oss's sake, I made myself lean forward to peer at the tiny face peeking out of the soiled towels.

It was clear right away why they'd chosen to have a home birth with only a single unlucky midwife for help. The baby took exclusively after her mother: strange dark eyes, same translucent skin, and a full set of sharp little teeth. I swallowed, unable to speak.

"Do you want to hold her?"

I didn't have the heart to tell him no, I did not want to touch his weird new baby, but I didn't have to. The moment Oss reached for her, his wife hissed and twisted away. The humming deepened into a growl. Oss didn't recoil so much as snap away from the bed. His movements in that moment were weirdly robotic, not his own. It was like he'd been pushed away by some unseen force. The bedside lamp flickered and died. I backed into the dresser against the wall, remembering the spark of electricity that passed between us the first time I met Oss's wife. The flowers fell onto the carpet as I fled.

After that, the color began to come into Oss's wife, if you can call it that. It started in her cheeks, and quickly spread—a sort of ash-gray, but still an improvement over the pallid quality of before. On the other hand, Oss seemed to fade a little each time I saw him. I took it upon myself to check on him regularly. I never liked the idea of him living alone with her in that house, sleeping next to her every night. Now there were two of them and Oss was outnumbered. She could do anything to him and no one would know until it was too late.

One day, I was over for dinner. Oss was in the kitchen cooking stir-fry. I passed by their bedroom on my way back from the bathroom, and noticed the door was open a crack. That same unsettling hum was coming from inside. A prickle crept up the back of my neck. I couldn't help myself. I peeked.

She had the baby on the bed, dripping something dark and thick into its mouth with her hand. I blinked, uncomprehending. What was I looking at? All at once, the grisly panorama crashed over me with merciless clarity.

Oss's wife held a small, decapitated animal upside down in her hand. A rodent. I recognized it by the thin, limp tail hanging over her thumb. She was feeding her infant its blood, carefully squeezing little drops one at a time so as not to choke it.

Then she saw me. The look she gave—not embarrassed or ashamed, but murderous. I had intruded on something I wasn't supposed to see. The bedside lamp sputtered with an electric hiss. She glanced down at my hand. I felt compelled to pull the door shut, turn around, and march back to the kitchen. I collapsed into a chair, staring at Oss's stir-fry. He knew something was wrong, but I couldn't find the words to tell him. She never did join us for dinner that night.

Oss called me one day in the spring, frantic. They'd had a fight. Afterward, she'd taken the baby out for a walk, whatever that meant. I was shocked at his appearance when he opened the door for me. He'd lost more weight. His jeans and flannel shirt hung off his frame. The skin clung to the bones of his face. She'd made him into a little old man, tired and bent. He leaned against the door frame in what was supposed to be a casual stance, but I knew it was because he was out of breath.

Still, I wasn't prepared for what I saw inside the house: kitchen drawers ripped from the wall, utensils scattered across the linoleum with the sharp remnants of broken dishes, cupboards hanging off their hinges. Someone had slashed open the secondhand couch cushions and strewn the stuffing all over the living room floor. The antique upright piano was smashed in, the bench overturned.

"Oss, what happened in here?"

He barely glanced at the chaos around us. "I want to show you something." He led me to the downstairs cellar. Despite the worn, brick walls and the exposed beams supporting the floor above, Oss had managed to turn this tiny, cold room into a decent man-cave for his projects. It was the only space in the house that belonged to him. He pulled the string to a bare bulb hanging from the ceiling. There was a workbench with a table saw set up along one wall. He went to a giant tool chest in the corner and grasped the edges. I grabbed the other end, and together we slid it away from the corner, revealing a hole in the packed dirt floor beneath. Oss bent down, lifted a wooden box the size of an old-fashioned doctor's satchel out of the hole, and hefted it onto the work bench. He braced his hands against the surface while he caught his breath. For a moment, I thought he might pass out, but then he seemed to recover. He fished a metal key out of his jeans pocket and clicked open the heavy padlock on the front of the box.

Opening the lid, he reached inside. His actions were deliberate, careful, almost ceremonial. He lifted out a soft bundle, cradling it as he set it down next to the box. He beckoned me to come closer. Reluctantly, I stepped to the work bench as he gently unwrapped the cloth. Inside was a dark sheet of. . .something.

"What is that?" I asked.

Oss picked it up, unfolding it accordion-style to its full length. He held it draped across his arms so the ends spilled down his sides, about five feet in all. I could tell it had some weight to it, more substantial than cloth, but less so than leather. He moved it back and forth and it shimmered like a black rainbow, even in the anemic light of the bulb, iridescent blues, greens, and purples. He picked up a regular plastic spray bottle and used it to wet the surface. Then he polished the sheet with a cotton rag.

"Can't let it dry out," he said.

"Oss," I persisted. "What is that thing?"

He looked up at me then, his eyes bright and hopeful behind the glasses perched on his skeletal face.

"Her skin," he told me, as though it were obvious. He held it out to me. "You can touch it if you want." I shook my head, backing away. He took a step closer. "It's okay. I don't mind." I threw up my hands, feeling the dry air between us crackle. Static electricity bit at my fingertips, made my hair stand on end. The same awful power Ossman's wife held over him also manifested in this thing he kept hidden like some bizarre trophy.

"Get it away from me!"

His expression collapsed, hurt. He laid the sheet onto the workbench. "I found it that day, by the river. I have to keep it safe."

"Why?"

He blinked. He was having difficulty with an answer, which only worried me more. "Because. . .if I don't, she'll leave. She'll take my little girl and I'll never see them again."

"Was she. . .looking for it?"

Oss just shrugged, as though the aftermath right above our heads was no more sinister than the mess left by a child's birthday party.

I tried not to betray my growing desperation. "Hey, Oss. Why don't you come stay with me for a while?"

He actually laughed. "And leave my family? Come on."

"Just for a few days. Until this blows over."

He continued casually as though I hadn't spoken, brushing the edge of the sheet with his fingers. "You know, I never see her feed the baby. But she must be, right?"

I swallowed the bile rising in my throat. The light bulb began to buzz. Oss's head snapped up, his eyes wide. In an instant, his expression flashed to panic.

"She's home!" His hands shook as he rushed to wrap up the dark sheet and return it to the box. "You can't tell her about this." I heard the front door open and close upstairs. Oss stumbled to the corner, lowering the box back into the earth. Something glinted on the surface of the workbench. The key. While Oss's back was turned, I stuffed it into my jacket pocket. I followed him to the corner where I helped him shove the tool chest back over the hole.

Oss gripped my arms. "Promise me you won't say anything," he whispered. "Please! She can never find out where it is."

The pleading in his voice scared me. This woman had turned my childhood friend, who'd once hiked through the Andes just to volunteer at a remote orphanage for three months, who never batted an eye at skydiving or free rock climbing, into a paranoid shell. I hated her for it. "Okay, buddy. I promise."

I watched him relax. He released his death-grip on my arms. "I know. I'm sorry. You're a good friend."

"Come home with me, Oss. Just for tonight. You're not safe here."

"Nah," he smiled, all nonchalance again. "We'll be fine. We'll work it out."

She was waiting at the top of the stairs with the child.

By that time she was walking, and never left her mother's side. I paused in the stairwell. They just stared down at me, unblinking. I nodded politely, and continued to the front door, feeling both of them watch me like those creepy hologram Halloween decorations with the eyes that follow you wherever you go. The goosebumps erupted on my skin the moment I stepped onto the porch.

Driving home, I couldn't help wondering, would it be such a bad thing if she left with her unnatural baby and Oss never had to see them again? If he wasn't going to leave that house, maybe she should. My Scottish grandmother told us stories about selkies, seals who turned into beautiful women once they stepped onto land and shed their seal-skins. The best way to catch one was to hide her skin. She couldn't return to the ocean without it. A selkie could live for years on land, but once she found her skin, she'd run back to the water where she belonged.

Seals were graceful, charming, even cute. Oss's wife was none of those things. Last I checked, there were no wild seals in the Snake River. No, she was. . .something else. I thought of the dark, unsettling beauty of the skin Oss had shown me, and realized what each of those different colors represented. Scales.

Oss was still a young guy. He could move on, remarry when the time was right. Most importantly, he would be safe from her.

The next morning, I knocked on Oss's door. He was at work, as I'd hoped, but she was home. The door cracked open and one of her giant, black eyes peeked out to evaluate me. I held up the key.

"The cellar," I said. "Under the tool chest." The eye flicked down to the key. Then a gray hand snaked out, snatched it from my fingers, and slammed the door in my face.

That night, I dreamed about her feeding the baby. But in my dream, the tiny, decapitated animal in her hand was Oss. I bolted awake, cold dread pouring from me like sweat. I never should have left him there. I should have made him leave with me. It was still dark outside, but I flew out of bed and raced back to Oss's place.

The house was black when I arrived, immune to the street lamps' soft bubbles of light. I screeched to a stop at the curb and pounded on the front door for what felt like several minutes, but there was no answer. The only sound was the water flowing over the rocks in the creek behind the house. I backed up onto the grass and shouted Oss's name at his bedroom window, but still the house stayed dark.

I returned to the front door and kicked at it until I broke through. The inside felt like a tomb. The kitchen had been partially cleaned up, with drawers stacked on the countertop and the spilled utensils tossed inside. A single half-eaten plate of food sat abandoned on the kitchen table. I took the stairs two at a time.

"Oss?" I called.

The bedroom door was ajar. I pushed it open, afraid of what I would find, but there was no one inside. By the light of the bedside lamp, I saw Oss's wooden box sitting in the middle of the floor, like it was waiting for me. I knelt down and sucked in a breath.

Fingertips stuck out from under the lid.

I grasped the edge, flipped it back, and stumbled away.

Oss stared back at me from inside the box, motionless, folded in on himself. All contorted limbs and twisted spine, one hand tucked up under his chin, one eye half-open, the pale face stretched across his skull, petrified in an expression of shock and pain. Only at the end did he see what she really was.

I began to scream. At first, the only part of me that worked was my voice. Then my arms were dragging me back to the bedroom doorway. Finally, my legs, like jelly, came up beneath me so I could stumble back down the stairs and out the front door just in time to vomit over the porch rail into the dead flower bed. I fumbled in my pocket for my cell phone to dial 911 with shaking fingers.

Halfway to my car, an electric jolt sent my entire body rigid. I crashed onto the front lawn, rolling onto my back. I lay there, paralyzed. Only my eyes would move, but I heard soft footsteps approaching in the grass. She appeared in the corner of my eye, her face moving closer and closer, until she filled the whole scope of my vision.

She knelt over me. Her dark hair, haloed against the light of the street lamps, dripped water onto my face. She was changing before my eyes, becoming more eel-like with every breath. Her eyes seemed to grow bigger and blacker, moving farther and farther apart. Her nose flattened, disappearing into the gray skin above her lipless mouth.

More movement on my other side. The child lurked a few feet away. She was changing too, just like her mother. She watched me impassively, cocking her head to the side as though she was only mildly curious. I looked back to Oss's wife. Pins and needles buzzed along my arms and legs. My fingers twitched. Whatever she had done to me, the effect was wearing off, but not quick enough to save me from whatever she planned to do next.

My friend was dead long before she stuffed him into that box. He was dying the moment he met her. Giving her the key had only killed him faster. Now it was my turn.

She leaned in, softly touching my cheek. Little crackles of electricity popped along my skin under her damp fingertips. Her breathing had grown ragged, drawing in great gulps of air through her mouth now that her nostrils had ceased to exist. She shuddered, and I watched a trio of pulsing gills slit open down her neck, as though drawn by a scalpel. She held up her fist, clutching the shimmery sheet of her skin. As the wail of a siren approached in the distance, she smiled down at me with a row of piscine teeth: *Thank you.*

She stepped over me, swept the child into her arms, and disappeared toward the creek in a silent flash, leaving me frozen and helpless in the grass, even long after the spell had worn off.

My friend Oss liked to brag about how he'd gone fishing in the Snake River and caught a wife instead, but I knew. It was always the other way around.

Resister

Lehua Parker

When Alicia Brown spotted Reginald "Monty" Montgomery's black Jag roaring through Serenity Circle, she dropped her Cosmo next to the emergency bottle of Grey Goose and ran for the coffee pot.

She poured a fresh cup—two Splendas, no cream—just as Monty, Senior Funeral Director and Chairman of the Board, blew into the foyer of Montgomery Mortuary, One and Done, Our Promise for Over 50 Years.

"What the hell, Alicia?" he griped, waving his cell phone. "You know Thursdays are golf days. I was just about to birdie on the 8th. I had the Mayor in the palm of my hand."

She held out the mug. "Sorry, Mr. Montgomery, but this can't wait. We've got a Resister."

Monty rolled his eyes and took a healthy slug. "Resisters are Reggie's department. Call him."

"I did, but he's had a minor fender-bender with the hearse."

"With a Resister in the back?"

"No, Reggie couldn't get—"

"Wait. The Resister's loose?"

"No, it's okay." Alicia jerked her head toward the morgue. "She's chilling in the cooler. The husband and some guy brought her in."

"Damn it, Alicia! For a second I thought we had a real problem." Monty rubbed his chest. "You know I got a weak heart."

"Sorry, Mr. Montgomery. I called because the situation's a bit delicate."

"Oh?" Monty said, sipping his coffee.

"She's a repeat."

"What?" Monty choked. "We haven't had a two-fer in over a decade. It's right there in our brochure!"

"Technically, she's a three-fer," Alicia said.

"Three?" Monty put the coffee down and picked up the paperwork. "What's our exposure? Missing children? Pets?"

Alicia shook her head. "Nothing on the police scanner."

"Doorbell footage? Witnesses?"

"I don't think so. Nothing on the news."

"Hallelujah for small favors. Where's the husband?"

"In the Consolation Room. They've been waiting over an hour. But there's something off about the second guy. He's twitchy. Like he has an ax to grind."

Monty frowned. "You think the husband lawyered-up?"

"I'm not sure."

"JC Penny suit? Scuffed pleather loafers?"

"No, wrinkled khakis and a golf shirt, no logo. He's not one of the regular hearse-chasers."

"Probably a CSI wannabe." Monty sighed, scanning pages. "This crapfest just gets better and better."

Alicia hefted the coffee pot. "Refill?"

"No, I better get in there." Monty adjusted his tie. "Straight?"

"Yeah. Turn," Alicia said, running a lint brush across his shoulders. "You're good. No dandruff. Mint?"

Monty popped it into his mouth and chewed. "Thanks. I can't believe Reggie botched this so badly." He snapped the file closed. "I'm taking today's green fees out of his paycheck—that'll teach him."

"Mr. Montgomery, just one more thing—I lit candles, but we're gonna have to steam clean."

"Again? Can't you just—"

"Nope. There's not enough Febreze in the world," Alicia said. "Three times in seven months. Can you imagine?"

"No, and neither can you. Resisters don't happen at Montgomery Mortuary. It's right there on the wall—one and done."

"Of course. Should I call Durfy's? See if they can get a cleaning crew out here before lunch?"

"What do you think? I'm already handling Reggie's mess; I'm not doing your job, too," he said, striding down the hall.

When Monty entered the room, the first thing he noticed was five floral candles burning on the credenza. The second was the strong wave of graveyard stench emanating from the soiled tee-shirt of the man rising from his chair.

Monty held out his hand. "Good morning. I'm Reginald Montgomery. I'm so sorry for your loss."

"Thank you," said the man. "I'm Marcus Palmer."

A trained professional, Monty didn't grimace when the hand he shook had the distinct slime of corpse wax clinging to it, though his stomach lurched and his eyes went straight to the industrial-sized bottle of Purell and box of tissues on the conference table.

"Sorry," Mark said. "This stuff is hard to clean off."

"Not at all, not at all. We see this all the time with the Resistant. It's entirely natural and nothing to be embarrassed about." Monty dropped the file on the table and pumped hand-sanitizer like he believed it actually worked.

Monty nodded to the other man. "Under the circumstances, I think we can dispense with handshaking."

"Good, 'cause I wouldn't shake your hand anyway," he said. "You owe us, Montgomery. Big time."

"Bernie—" Mark said.

"No, Mark. What they did ain't right. We ought to sue."

Monty tossed a handful of tissues in the trash and filled his palm again. "And you are?"

"Your worst nightmare!" snarled the man in the slept-in clothes.

Monty looked at Mark, eyebrow raised.

Mark grabbed the man's arm. "Easy, Bernie," he hissed. "Remember, we want him on our side." Louder, he said, "Sorry, Mr. Montgomery. This is my brother-in-law,

Bernard Jamison. He's a little distraught."

"So I see." Monty flipped the file open. "As the deceased's brother—"

"Oh, no, no. Martha was an only child. Bernie's married to my sister, Karen. Karen's watching my kids, Daniel and Grace," Mark said.

"Ah," Monty said. "Well, emotional support—"

Bernie said, "I'm not here for emotional support, pal. I keep track of where the bodies ain't buried, if you know what I mean."

Monty's eyes narrowed. "Are you a lawyer, Mr. Jamison?"

"Maybe," Bernie said. "Maybe not. You shaking in your boots yet, Mr. Big Shot Undertaker?"

Monty sighed. "Positively shivering," he muttered. "Mark—may I call you Mark?"

"Sure. And he's Bernie."

"Nope. Only my friends call me Bernie."

"Really, Bernie?" Mark said. "You're going there?"

"Fine. He can call me Bernie. Sheesh."

"Excellent. Please call me Monty."

Mark said, "Monty, the lady in the front said you're the guy in charge, the one who makes decisions."

"That's me." Monty pulled out a chair. "Let's sit down and discuss this like friends, shall we? What seems to be the problem?"

"Are you kidding me?" Mark said.

Monty gave him a blank look.

"We paid you good money—" started Bernie.

Monty held up his hand. "Let's just start at the beginning." He turned to the last page in the file. "Your wife, Martha Marie Palmer, maiden name Griswold, died seven months ago, on May 7th."

"That's right."

"The cause of death was acute chlorine gas poisoning." Monty paused. "How extraordinary. An industrial accident?"

"No. She was cleaning. She tripped on the bathmat and hit her head. The Windex fell into the bleach bucket. She never woke up."

"My condolences. It says she wasn't found for ten hours—is that right?"

Mark shrugged. "I was on the couch, watching TV. Martha was cleaning. She was always cleaning. I fell asleep and didn't wake up until morning—late for work and with a stiff neck. I found her when I went to—you know."

"No autopsy?"

"No. I refused, and the coroner agreed since the cause of death was obvious. Accidental acute chlorine gas poisoning. The bathroom door was shut."

Monty turned a page. "There are two receiving dates: one the afternoon of May 7th and another pre-dawn, May 12th. This was the Resister incident?"

"Yeah, the first one. There's been three."

"I'm so sorry. Resisters are very rare. Once in a blue moon."

"Yeah, I read your brochure," Mark said.

"Oh, good!" Monty said.

"Not like there was anything else to do while we waited," Bernie muttered.

Mark shot Bernie a warning look and cleared his throat. "We came to Montgomery Mortuary specifically because of your one and done reputation, Monty."

Monty nodded. "One and done is what our clients experience when they follow our recommendations. However, bodies are sometimes older than coroners estimate. Sometimes other factors come into play. We typically have a single Resister event every three years or so, well below national average, and never twice. Three times is unheard of. It might be a new state record. Martha is highly unusual."

"Yeah, well, the whole thing is hinky," Bernie said.

Monty held up a hand. "We'll get to your concerns in a moment, Bernie. Mark, take me through what happened on the twelfth."

Mark inhaled deeply and stared into space. "It was after midnight. The kids were asleep. I heard a noise in the kitchen. Pots banging, cupboards opening. I thought we had a burglar. I grabbed my gun—"

"Your gun?"

"Yeah, from my nightstand. I went downstairs. When I came into the kitchen, there she was, standing with the fridge open."

Monty nodded. "Eating raw hamburger?"

Mark shook his head. "No."

"Chicken breasts? Resisters lick frozen ones like popsicles."

"No, she was pulling out neighbors' casseroles, saying she needed to check them for cheese since Daniel can't have dairy. Gives him the runs."

Monty's eyes bulged. "What?"

"Yeah, on account he's lactose intolerant. He can't have milk, either, not even on cereal."

Monty waved his hand. "Not that. Martha talked?"

"Of course. She wouldn't shut up. Started doing the dishes and whining it's a good thing she's back since I was ruining the kids' teeth. Too many cookies and pies, she said. She asked if I'd signed Grace's permission slip for her fieldtrip. Told me she'd take Daniel to soccer practice tomorrow."

"That's incredible," Monty said, scribbling a note. "I've never heard of a coherent Resister. What happened next?"

"I told her she was dead. She just laughed—"

"Laughed?"

"Yeah, she laughed and said she knew, but didn't have time to be dead. Started nagging me about mowing the lawn."

"And then?"

"I'd had enough. I double-tapped."

"Double-tapped?"

Mark held his fingers like a gun. "Yeah. Pow-pow. Double-tap. One in the chest, then one in the head. Double-tap."

Nonplussed, Monty sat there for a second, scanning the file. "You shot her in the head?"

"Yeah."

"But she came back twice more?" Monty asked, shuffling papers.

"Well," Bernie drawled, "It was head-ish."

"Shut-up, Bernie. You weren't there," Mark said.

"What do you mean, head-ish?"

"Tell him," Bernie said.

Mark looked away.

"Tell him," Bernie said again. "He needs to know."

"All right! It was her jaw. The second bullet ran along her jaw and out the back of her throat." Mark glared. "Happy now, Bernie?"

Bernie patted Mark's arm. "It's okay. It's still a double -tap in my book."

"So, not really in the head," Monty said. "That makes sense." He tuned a page. "After the," air quotes, "double-tap, what happened?"

"She went down. I ran around the counter and picked her up. She was stunned and didn't kick much. There wasn't any blood."

"No, there wouldn't be. Her heart wasn't pumping."

"I panicked. She started to come around, started making weird noises. I worried she'd wake the kids."

"But the gunshots…" Monty trailed off, then shook his head. "Never mind. Continue, please."

"I threw her into the pantry and braced a kitchen chair under the doorknob. I called the mortuary's after-hours number, and not five minutes later, Reggie and his assistant, Barry, roll up in a hearse."

"Laundry? You didn't tell me that," Bernie said.

"Yeah, well, I found my shirts in the dryer later. It's not important."

"Did she remember the Bounce?"

"Yeah."

"Well, that's Martha for you."

"Gentlemen, let's stay focused," Monty said. "You know why Resisters rise in places like California? Because those places don't embalm."

Bernie opened his mouth, but Monty waved his hand, cutting him off. He pointed to the file. "Regardless, Mark signed here and initialed there, acknowledging the risks involved with his burial plan that were contrary to our recommendations. Really, as awful as this is, this is entirely your fault, Mark. You knew she was a Resister, and yet you still buried her in a cardboard coffin without a vault."

Bernie's fist slammed the table. "Vaults! Another racket, just like metal caskets. I told Mark not to spring for extras, but he caved when Reggie peer-pressured him into renting a special viewing casket for the service. 'You can't have your wife lying in a cardboard box,' Reggie said. 'What will people think?'"

Mark said, "I think Reggie may have been right about that one. Martha's parents would've—"

"Hush. It would've been fine. Nobody would've said boo. But thanks to the mortuary's incompetence, we couldn't have a viewing in the fancy, rented casket. Instead, we had to pay another fee to stuff it full of foam padding to muffle any sounds

Martha made. A closed casket, no viewing, and we still had to pay the make-up and hair styling fees! It's all a racket."

Monty closed his eyes until his pulse calmed enough for him to speak.

"Martha was prepped the day before, so yes, you had to pay that fee. Remember, everything was fine until Mark blew half her face to smithereens. His initials are next to decline cosmetic reconstruction and also here, acknowledging that an open casket is impossible. We did the best we could with what we had to work with."

Monty flipped a few pages and nodded. "Okay. I'll concede the unfortunate power outage contributed to the first Resistance incident. I'll refund you the make-up and hair styling fees."

"Thank you," Mark said.

"However, if you'd followed our recommendations, there absolutely wouldn't have been a second or third time. Knowing she was a determined Resister, it's unconscionable that you didn't at least bury her in a metal casket."

"Nope. Those are on you, too," Bernie said. "Tell him, Mark."

Mark scraped at a bit of corpse wax on his palm and said, "The second time was a night about a month after the funeral. I heard a noise. Thought maybe a dog or a raccoon had gotten into the trash. I went outside with a flashlight." He held up his hands, turning them over and over. "Martha had raked a big pile of leaves and was bagging them. The downstairs windows gleamed where she'd washed them, but there were bits of her fingers floating in the bucket. She'd worn them down to stubs digging herself from her grave. When she saw me, she turned, and started to say something, something about the flower beds, I think. It was hard to understand her with her tongue hanging and half her jaw gone."

"I'm sorry you had to see that," Monty said.

Mark tipped his head to the side and examined his cuticles, running his thumb along each nailbed. "I distracted her by throwing the flashlight. I grabbed a Hefty bag and threw it over her head. She struggled, leaves spilling left and right, but I managed to pick her up and get her into the garage. I tied her with Grace's jump rope and stuck her in the freezer, securing the lid with Daniel's bike lock. The kids were getting up soon, and I didn't want them to see her like that."

"Don't forget the roasts, Mark. They never reimbursed you for the roasts," Bernie said.

Monty flipped a page back and forth. "Roasts?"

"Mark had to empty the freezer to make room for Martha. That was good deer and elk meat, ruined by the time you guys got around to picking her up."

"Ah. Here it is. Melted. What a shame." Monty sighed. "Again, I'm sorry for the loss, but this isn't our problem. Mark put his wife in the freezer, not us. If he'd followed our recommendations for a metal coffin or a cement vault, he'd still have plenty of venison for Sunday dinner."

Bernie shook his head. "I disagree. What was he supposed to do? Invited her in to cook breakfast? How unhygienic is that?"

Monty checked his watch and stifled another sigh.

"Besides," Bernie continued, "she didn't come back the second time because of a cardboard coffin. She came back because you broke the law."

"Beg pardon?"

"You didn't bury her six feet deep."

Monty raised his head and looked down his nose. "At Montgomery Mortuary, we take pride in our burials. We use state of the art measuring tools which—by law, as you're so fond of saying—are certified and calibrated annually. There is no way we buried her less than six feet."

"Maybe not at first, but your crew still screwed up," Mark said. "Anything less than six feet is considered Resister-depth, and illegal. After Martha's second rising, I had Barry use your fancy tools. We measured the top of the casket at five feet, ten inches. He admitted that the fill dirt settled. You skimped and didn't compact properly. Want to see the pictures?"

Monty cleared his throat. "Dirt settles when cardboard caskets start to decompose. That's why we recommend metal coffins and vaults for peace of mind. I'm sorry, Mark. I feel for you and all that you've been through, but you must recognize you're at fault for both the second and third risings."

Monty turned the file toward Mark. "There's your signature approving the second burial plan with your initials acknowledging that it was against our recommendations and industry best practices. And here's the line item where we gave you a 50% discount on our least expensive wood coffin for the reburial. Half, Mark! That's barely above cost. And here's where we gave you full return credit for the original cardboard casket, even though it was performing exactly as specified. You wanted back to earth, right?"

Mark mumbled something indistinguishable and hung his head.

"And here, here's the invoice that shows, per your request in lieu of a metal coffin, we zip-tied her wrists to specially installed eyebolts and used sheetrock screws to secure the lid. We even reinterred her an extra two feet deep at no additional charge. We did all of this because we care, Mark. We really care."

Mark raised his head and swallowed. "But the bolts and screws didn't hold. This morning, I was sound asleep when I felt the bed dip. There was an indescribable stench, like wet dog rolled in fish guts. I turned to push Duke away and came face to face with—I can't. I just can't." He buried his face in his hands.

"Would you like some water?"

"No. I just want this over. In my mind, I keep hearing Martha try to speak. It sounded like—it's so awful, I can't bear it. I think she was trying to say—"

"What?"

"Snuggle."

Mark burst into tears.

Monty stood up and opened the conference door. "Alicia?" he called. "Bring the Goose."

"Right away, Mr. Montgomery."

Bernie put his arm around Mark.

Mark hiccupped. "I had to touch her. I had to push her away. I leaped out of bed and threw the duvet—"

"Blanket," Bernie said.

"What?" Mark blinked.

"It was a blanket, not a duvet."

"Martha always called it a duvet."

"Martha was wrong."

Mark pressed his palms against his forehead.

Bernie shrugged. "Details. It's my blessing and a curse."

"Damn it, Bernie! You and your details and conspiracy theories! If I hadn't listened to you—"

"Whoa, I saved you hundreds of dollars! You wanna be somebody's death patsy—"

"Gentlemen, let's move on."

Mark said, "I rolled Martha in the duv—blanket, and put her in the trunk. I called Karen. Bernie and I drove here. The lady at the front desk called Barry. And here we are."

"You're sure you brought her back without witnesses, missing pets—"

"What?"

"Nothing. I mean, that's wonderful. Well done. Now that she's back, we have two options. Reinter using a metal casket or vault—"

"Nope. We're not falling for that," Bernie said.

"Or," Monty said, glaring at Bernie, "cremation."

"Cremation? Cook her in an oven like a…a…"

"Roast?" Bernie said.

"Shut up, Bernie," Mark said. "You're not helping."

"Geez, somebody got up on the grumpy side of the bed today."

Monty said, "Mark, I know this is hard for you. Martha's a deep Resister, but even she can't come back from cremation."

Bernie chimed in. "What about that guy in India? The one in all the papers last year. The one who ate his neighbor's cat."

"A hoax. Even the hardline Resurrectionists agree that never happened. Trust me, Mark. Cremation is safe and effective."

"When?" Mark asked.

"As soon as this afternoon. We have two already scheduled—that will allow you to split the preheat fees three ways."

"Oh, goodie," Mark said. "More fees."

"You'll need an urn. We have a lovely selection. I'm sure we can find something that will look great on your mantle."

"Hold your horses, Mr. Let's-Cremate-When-We've-Already-Paid-for-a-Plot-and-a-Coffin-and-Rented-a-Fancy-Casket-for-a-Viewing!" Bernie huffed. "You're double-dipping. Amazing. How do you live with yourself?"

Monty said, "Bernie, for the last time—"

Mark held up a hand. "No, I want to hear what Bernie has to say."

"Here's how they get you, Mark. When somebody doesn't let them rip him off with all their fancy add-ons, they induce Resistance by warming the corpse and let it escape right before the funeral, hoping that will scare him into paying exorbitant fees for things he doesn't need. When that doesn't work, they don't bury the coffin deep enough, so the Resister rises again. But if he still doesn't cave, they sabotage the second burial by using substandard zip ties and don't wire the mouth. They've been in the death business long enough to know that eventually the hands are going to pull free from the wrists, and the Resister will gnaw their way out. The new coffin? It's wood all right—balsa wood. And now, at the third rising, they try to up-sell again. Cremate the Resister, it's the only way—and at full price when it's less than half its original weight."

Bernie brushed one index finger with the other. "For shame, Monty, for shame."

Monty sat back in his chair.

"That's an interesting story, Bernie, but here's the truth. Montgomery Mortuary's been taking care of the dead for over fifty years. Someday my son Reggie will take over the business my father started. We understand how difficult it is to lose someone. It's even harder to have them come back. That's why we pride ourselves on one and done. But unless you take our advice, Mark, Martha will come back. She'll keep trying until something stops her. She's not your typical Resister motivated by revenge or a desire for brains. She's motivated by love."

Bernie said, "Love? That's a new one. Mark, maybe it's not such a good thing that Carol wasn't there this morning."

"Bernie! We're not official. The kids don't know."

Bernie zipped his lips and threw away the key. "Your secret's safe with me. But if Martha had found Carol on her side of the bed, maybe she wouldn't be so hot to come back."

"Bernie."

"Yeah, Mark?"

"Just stop. Please."

"Whatever you need, Mark. I'm here for you."

"Monty, how much?"

"Cremation?" Monty pulled a calculator from his suit coat. "There's the base fee plus a third of the preheat. I'll waive the rush and the prep fees."

"Mighty kind of you," Mark said. "Are you throwing in a car wash, too?"

"Ha! You're a funny man, Mark. I'll get you Durfy's number. If anyone can get the smell out of your trunk, they can. Tell 'em Monty sent you, and they'll give you the WIFI password for free."

"Amazing."

"But back to Martha. Do you want to inter the urn in the grave or do you want a refund credit—twenty percent of the plot's purchase price, less clean up fees?"

"Twenty percent? That's robbery!" Bernie said.

"It's a used grave, Bernie. It's not worth a tenth of the original price, especially since I'm required to disclose that the original occupant was a Resister. People are superstitious. Even Resurrectionists get spooked. I'm doing you a solid here by offering you twenty percent."

"What's the damage? Rock-bottom," Mark asked.

Monty punched a few numbers. "Urn?"

"No."

"What about the ashes?"

Mark thought for a moment. "You got a manila envelope?"

"Yes."

"Let's go with that."

After number crunching, Monty said, "Cremation, including plot credit and original beauty fee refunded, cremains placed in an 11x13 envelope, comes to $8,495.27. That's the best I can do."

Mark paused. "What if I provide the envelope?"

Monty pressed a few buttons on the calculator and squinted at the result. "That'd make it $8,495.12. Doesn't save much. I buy envelopes in bulk."

Mark propped his head in his hands and sighed. "How much to simply rebury Martha in her grave?"

"A metal casket or vault's going to cost more."

"We don't need them. I saw her stubby arms. Her teeth were worn down to nubs. She could barely walk. It's not going to be easy for her to rise again. How much to wire her mouth, bind her arms and legs to her body with layers of Saran wrap, and bury her face down?"

Bernie said, "Perfect! She'll dig the wrong way!"

"You're both mad."

"And what if we filled the casket with plaster?" Mark said.

"Like a cement vault, but inside," Bernie crowed. "Brilliant!"

"How much for that, Monty?"

Monty cleared the calculator and muttered, "Reinternment, plus wire and plastic wrap, plus plaster of Paris, plus three days cooler storage, plus time and labor, minus make-up and hair refund. And since I'm feeling generous, minus a 15% frequent flyer discount. Add tax. That's $8,365.53. You save $129.59 over cremation. But I cannot recommend this. She'll find a way to come back."

"Of course you don't like it—you lose money," Bernie said. "Mark's a disrupter. He's the Uber and Airbnb of funerals. It's the wave of the future, Monty, and it's coming for you."

"Gentlemen, you're not thinking clearly. Money isn't the issue. It's peace of mind. It's the— "

"What? The law? The law doesn't require embalming or metal caskets or vaults. It doesn't require cremation—not even for Resisters. I want a simple, natural burial for my wife."

"But the risks—"

"No buts," Mark said. "Write it up. I'll sign your waiver again. And I want my duvet back, too."

"Blanket."

"Whatever, Bernie."

Monty grabbed the file and stood. "This your final decision?"

"Yes."

"You're sure I can't change your mind?"

"I'm sure."

Alicia knocked, then entered carrying a tray.

"Thank you, Alicia. Please, help yourselves while I get the paperwork started. Alicia, come with me."

"How'd it go," Alicia whispered.

"Swimmingly. They want to do a pump and dump. And get this—they want to use plaster of Paris."

"What? Three risings and they still didn't go for cremation or a vault?"

"Nope. Not even a metal casket. I was wrong about Reggie botching the upsell. These guys are a goldmine. Bringing her back a third time was genius."

Alicia grinned.

"Make sure Reggie uses the good plastic wrap. Otherwise, it'll be a bitch to chip the body from the plaster."

"Got it. When?"

"Let's schedule number four in a month. Christmases should be memorable."

"The 24th?"

"No, that's staff family time. Make it the 23rd."

"Done."

"And put her in a Santa hat. It'll be our little joke."

"Oh, you're so bad, Mr. Montgomery! You think the fourth time's going to be the charm?"

"Oh, I hope not. The Jag needs new tires."

Night Watch

Madeline M. Marcum

Moonlight filtered into The Girl's bedroom through a set of short gossamer curtains. Shadows cast by the furniture overlapped, shading the floor and walls in various depths of darkness.

On the other side of the room The Girl lay in bed, knees close to her chest. Her sleepy gaze drifted along the white painted bed frame until it rested on Kiri, the plush brown bunny that she'd had since she was a toddler. The fur was faded in patches and one black glass eye was badly scratched. Comforted by the toy in its usual spot tucked up onto the corner of her headboard, she pulled her comforter tight around her chin. Soon she drifted off on the gentle waves of untroubled sleep.

The stale air in the toy chest was unpleasant to breathe. Bakko wasn't sure how long he'd been awake this time, but it was long enough that he'd become uncomfortable, wedged between a stiff horse and a plastic castle. He was grateful when Kiri opened the lid and helped him out. His embroidered nose detected the plush bunny's familiar scent of old patchouli fabric softener as they dropped to the hardwood floor.

"I hope tonight's the night you learn to use your magic." Kiri studied him with her good eye. "Looks like you're going to get to fight your first fiend."

Bakko's round ears drooped. "Really? Are you sure?"

"Yes, my dear bear," she said crisply. "Can't you feel it? The magic warning you?"

Kiri had told him that a clear tingling would alert him when a hunting fiend was close by. Now there was, and he felt nothing. He knew admitting that would only give Kiri more reason to be disappointed at his apparent ineptitude.

"I feel it," he fibbed.

It was difficult for Bakko to sense anything other than Kiri's exasperation that he still couldn't use the innate magic all Guardians possessed to protect children; their entire purpose for existing, he'd been told. After being awake for three nights, Bakko wasn't entirely sure what she'd meant.

"Good." One of Kiri's tall ears twitched. "Now, I bet we only have a couple of minutes, but let's have you give it a try anyway." Folding her legs underneath her, she sat down.

Attempting to match her gracefulness, Bakko carefully lowered himself across from his mentor. Kiri held out her paws. Golden-hued light appeared, spreading over them. Little by little, the light crept up her arms and down her torso until her entire figure glowed.

Although she'd demonstrated using magic many times before, he was still stunned by the brilliant display. Warmth radiated from her in invisible ripples. Bakko couldn't deny that he envied the way Kiri effortlessly guided the magic; it was part of her in a way that was utterly foreign to him. He self-consciously regarded his own lackluster pink form.

She rested her paws on her legs, the magic fading from sight.

"Let's have you try again, Bakko." Kiri gestured at the bed. "Remember, we don't just sit around and look scary, we have a job to do."

Bakko glanced up where the child that Kiri had called The Girl dreamed. Squelching the doubts that crowded his mind, he closed his eyes and inhaled deeply to help soothe his nerves.

"Hey," Kiri said.

"Wait," Bakko whispered, "let me have a few seconds."

Kiri grabbed his shoulder. "No. You're out of time."

"What?" Bakko opened his eyes.

"Look."

Following Kiri's pointed paw, Bakko noticed a border of gold magic glowing around the window. The line pulsed, dimming with each quaver.

Kiri huffed. "Practice will have to wait, if you live." She reached under the bed and pulled out a long, red ribbon. Paws glowing, she snapped the ribbon out to its full length, magic spreading along the band. "You don't want to sit there. Fiends can use the darkest shadows as camouflage to move through a room. Whatever's coming through the window could pop up right behind you."

Bakko scrambled to his feet and hurried to share a patch of moonlight with Kiri.

A cloud of panic engulfed him. There was so little he knew about the approaching menace, only that they had an insatiable hunger for the acute growing life force in children. Bakko's thoughts raced. He was about to face a fiend, powerless to protect himself.

The magic around the window disappeared in a puff.

Dread pounded in Bakko's temples. He scanned the room, straining to distinguish anything out of the ordinary in the remote, dark corners. It bothered him how much he could hear his own breathing. If he could hear it, he was certain that whatever was coming through the window could too.

The hush was split by a piping chittering around the bed frame. The irregular sound raised the fur on his back.

Kiri and Bakko clambered up the toy chest and onto the foot of the bed. Another barrier of magic glowed around the mattress. Between that and the veiled moonlight, Bakko could make out the fiend. His ears turned down.

It had no eyes, its only discernible feature a maw spanning the entire width of its amorphous body. Bent rows of glistening sharp teeth kept the mouth from closing. Four spindly arms protruded from the fiend's treacly sides, each ending in razor talons.

Tremors palpitated through the barrier as the fiend reached for The Girl, its oily hide spasming every time one of its claws was repelled.

The Girl slept with the lavender comforter wrapped tightly around her, ignorant of the monstrosity clawing at the edge of her bed.

Instinct roared at Bakko to crawl back into the toy chest. He swallowed, his dry throat making a gulping noise.

At the sound, the eyeless fiend turned toward the Guardians. Its maw stretched impossibly far as it let out a gurgling growl.

Kiri raised her ribbon and charged at the fiend. She only made it a few bounds before it noticed her.

Staring at the creature that was at least ten times his size, Bakko stayed rooted as if he'd grown from the quilted bed cover. He watched on in terror as Kiri ducked under the fiend's slashing claws. She rammed into it feet first, sending the fiend rocking back. Kiri cracked the ribbon down on its head, each blow of the glowing weapon leaving a smoking crater.

A whining screech rattled past the creature's curved teeth.

Kiri yelled, "Bakko!" The fiend's claws whirred around her.

His mentor's cry shook him from his petrified stupor. Bakko pushed instinct aside and ran to join the fray. He made it to the edge of the bed just as a claws rose behind Kiri. Not giving himself time to think better of it, Bakko launched at the fiend, crashing into its claws.

It released a feral scream and whipped its arm, nearly flinging Bakko into The Girl's wide night stand. The fiend lashed him back and forth as Kiri flayed it with her ribbon. Closing his eyes against the odor of mildew and decay emanating from its open maw, he clung to the claw with all the tenacity he could muster.

"Use your magic!" Kiri shouted.

Bakko would have laughed if he hadn't thought it would loosen his grip. He'd never been able to use magic when he had been calm and concentrating. Bakko couldn't believe that Kiri had the nerve to ask him to try at that very moment.

All at once the fiend's thrashing slowed, its shuddering sending ripples over its inky skin. Bakko gasped when the claw he clenched to his chest vanished, sending him and Kiri into a freefall down to the floor.

Kiri grumbled under her breath as she helped him to his feet.

"Did we do it?" He stared at where the fiend had been. "Did we kill it?"

"No, it's hiding in the shadows. A shame too, I almost had that filthy thing dead."

Kiri stepped cautiously toward the night stand, keeping her ribbon ready.

Bakko was about to follow her, but decided to search elsewhere. He peered at the closet door. If he were a fiend, he would have slid under there, somewhere safe and dark.

Pain flared along his back as he was hurled to the ground.

"Bakko!"

A shrill screech erupted as the fiend rematerialized. Bakko tried to push himself up, but fell when his right arm flopped limply at his side. He cried out as stuffing spilled from the seam.

"Over here!"

Kiri pitched herself at the fiend, her ribbon raised. Bursting with magic, she brought her weapon down on the distracted fiend's head with a crack that cut deep into its bulging dome. Smoke billowed from the creature as it lost cohesiveness, its remains dribbling into a puddle of dark sludge that trickled through the floorboards. Bakko's stomach turned at the gruesome scene.

Fighting queasiness, he cradled his severed limb, looking away from the stuffing hanging outside of him. Kiri stood with her paws on her knees next to the disappearing puddle.

"Congrats," she said between gasps. "You lived."

Bakko sunk back with a moan.

±Δ±

It was impossible not to flinch every time Kiri pulled the stitches in Bakko's shoulder tight while he sat on the edge of the bed. She tugged at the needle at one last time.

"There," she said, "how's that?"

He rotated his shoulder, hesitating when the stitches pulled.

"Over time it'll loosen up." Kiri cut through the thread with a seam ripper. "Glad I kifed this handy sewing kit."

Bakko picked at stuffing fibers tangled in his pink fur.

He was aware of Kiri's eyes boring into the back of his head.

"Bakko, are you mad at me?"

"No." Bakko stared at the spot where the fiend had liquefied. A handful of droplets were all that remained. "Maybe a little." He kept his gaze down. "Why didn't you tell me more about fiends before tonight? You knew that we'd fight one sooner or later."

Bakko was surprised when Kiri didn't instantly retort. She groaned softly and joined him on the edge of the bed.

"You're right. I'm sorry. I did choose you after all."

Hearing Kiri's admission shocked Bakko.

Recovering, he asked, "Why did you though? You seem to do fine watching after The Girl on your own." He met her half-scored stare.

"It's hard to explain, but you'll eventually understand." Kiri rubbed at a thinning patch of fur on her leg. For the first time, Bakko noticed that her spotted appearance was actually wear and tear.

"The magic tells you things in a way, almost as if your intuition becomes clearer. You'll have a notion and just intuitively know, deep down, what it's saying. Like when I knew that I needed to pass on the Guardian role. From the time we're awakened we have a limited amount of magic. If the fiends don't get you, there comes a point when it runs out, and you'll just not wake up anymore."

Her words chilled Bakko to his stuffing. "Is that going to happen to you?"

Kiri nodded. "Yep, that's why I chose you to replace me."

Bakko sprung to his feet and tugged at his ears. "You can't! I need your help! I can't go up against these fiends alone."

"Relax." She leaned back on her paws. "I've had years to prepare for this, that's why I'm training you."

The way Kiri talked about it so matter-of-factly appalled Bakko. Even though waking came with the task of battling nightmarish things, he wasn't sure he would ever find peace with the idea of having his life end.

"The fiends," he said, changing the subject. "Are they all like the one we fought tonight?"

Kiri sighed. "No, unfortunately. There are a few kinds you'll have to deal with. My predecessor only mentioned one other that I've never encountered. He called it the Guardian's worst enemy. I was told that they're pretty rare and don't go hunting as often." She shifted her weight uncomfortably. "Not that I ever wanted to meet it. The only time I saw him afraid was when he talked about that fiend."

That something worse than the fiend he had already faced might be in his future called back the urge to burrow into the toy chest and never come out again. Anything that could unsettle an experienced Guardian was something to be feared.

Bakko found it hard to swallow again.

"But what if I can't learn?" he asked softly. "What if I'm never able to use the magic?"

Kiri was quiet for some time.

"I don't know," she said.

Without magic, Bakko knew that it wouldn't be long before he was picked off by a fiend that decided to hurt The Girl. Bakko looked over at the sleeping child. She had no idea what odious things prowled her room at night. Then there was Kiri. Her shortness with him made sense; she was trying to help him on limited time—time that could run out at any moment. If he wasn't successful in learning how to be a Guardian, then the thousands of nights she'd spent fighting to protect The Girl would be for nothing.

Renewed resolve burned in Bakko's chest. Although she hadn't said it outright, Kiri needed him. No matter what, no matter how many fiends he had to contend with, he would make sure Kiri was glad she chose him.

Bakko's breath caught as golden light unfurled over him. Through the luminous haze he saw Kiri stand, her shock mirroring his own. With a little directing, Bakko guided the magic to his paws. They gleamed brightly with the concentrated power.

"Hey! Look at that," Kiri beamed. "You did it!"

He raised his paws and examined them curiously. "I guess I did."

±A±

Bakko felt like a new stuffed bear. Opportunities for him to explore his newfound ability had not been lacking over the past few nights.

"Hurry!" Kiri yelled as she struggled to keep her footing on the varnished floor.

Her ribbon was wrapped around a thick, black tentacle, one of many that knotted together to create the fiend that had slid under the bedroom door.

It wasn't the tentacles that bothered Bakko, it was the mouth full of gnashing teeth attached to the end of each of them. He'd nearly been bitten more than once when he'd forgotten to watch his back.

While Kiri held the wily creature in place, Bakko rushed forward with his weapon of choice: a yellow lead pencil with a string wrapped around it for a grip. At least five mouthed appendages darted at him, but he dropped and rolled out of their reach; one of the techniques that Kiri had taught him.

Bakko came to his feet and sent a burst of magic to his legs. Holding his glowing pencil above his head, he vaulted into the center of the tangled feelers. The fiend trembled as his pencil sank deep into the writhing mass. He managed to put a little distance between himself and the fiend before it began withering into infernal sludge.

Both Bakko and Kiri were breathing heavily while they watched the fiend disintegrate.

"Not bad, not bad," she puffed. "You've improved."

Unused to her complimenting him, even a little, Bakko rubbed at an imaginary scuff mark with his foot. There was a small part of him that was proud of how far he'd come. His impulse to flee or freeze at the sight of fiends had been steadily dwindling with every skirmish.

Kiri cleared her throat as her breath returned. "How's the stiff shoulder?"

Bakko barely noticed it anymore. Kiri had been right; it had loosened up over the course of a few days.

He was about to tell her so when the prickling behind his round ears startled him.

"Do you feel that too?" Bakko cocked his head.

Kiri's upright ears flicked attentively. "Yep. I feel it."

"Two in one night?"

"It happens." She didn't sound pleased. "Oh well. You know what to do."

Glowing weapon at the ready, Bakko hopped onto the bed. Placing a paw on the edge of the comforter like Kiri had taught him, he sent a burst of magic down his arm, reigniting the time-buying barrier around The Girl. Kiri joined him after she had done the same around the window and the door. Bakko caught the fresh scent of recently laundered sheets.

Silence settled over the bedroom like a fog.

"Where is it?" Kiri muttered, probing the bedroom with her unmarred eye. "I hate waiting for them to pop out of the shadows."

Bakko nodded in agreement. He'd learned to be wary of the deepest shadows in the room. It always caught him off guard when a fiend decided to materialize out of them. He wasn't sure he'd ever get used to it.

Scratching echoed in the bedroom.

"Where—" Bakko started to ask before he was shushed by Kiri.

More scratching. Bakko observed the magical barriers. None of them showed any sign of a fiend trying to cross.

Bakko gained Kiri's attention with a wave and pointed to the closet. Kiri shook her head in the negative. Her response was the same when he motioned to under the bed. Bakko took another sweep of the room, running through every possibility he could think of. He knew this was going to be a tricky one. Bakko's train of thought stopped abruptly. He tried unsuccessfully to avoid the answer he'd come to.

The scratching echoed louder.

He made eye contact with Kiri. Her uneasy expression told him that she'd arrived at the same conclusion. They both looked up.

Staring down from the ceiling was a fiend that appeared almost—human. Bakko's cry sat trapped in his throat at the horror above him. The creature's dark, wispy form adhered to the ceiling at the end of awkwardly hinged limbs. The head sitting on its shoulders bent unnaturally far against its back, staring straight down at Bakko and Kiri.

Bakko started to speak, but was interrupted when the fiend skittered across the ceiling and dropped to the foot of the bed. The fiend didn't make a sound as it crouched just inside the magical barrier, the joints in its arms and legs pointing in impossible directions.

Kiri cursed under her breath.

Bakko glanced at her for an explanation, but she was as shaken as he.

"I've never seen this before," she said.

Remembering that the only thing Kiri hadn't confronted was said to be their worst enemy sent a shiver through him.

Bakko gripped his sharpened pencil and pointed it at the fiend. He hoped that it wouldn't notice how the tip quivered.

Twisting its neck at a severe angle, the fiend focused on Bakko. No features adorned the smooth face except for a pair of overly large, watery eyes. The irises were a shocking blue. They made his nose itch.

"Let's flank it," Kiri directed, "I don't want to deal with this creep any longer than I have to."

Following her lead, Bakko moved slowly to the left. In his short experience, fiends would focus on one of them, giving him or Kiri the chance to strike the exposed side. But as he watched, Bakko sensed that this one wasn't like the others. One of its unblinking eyes followed him as he moved, the other followed Kiri, the space between the eyes increasing as they slid over the smoky visage. Bakko couldn't help staring at them. They made him uneasy, not only because they were uncanny, but because they were intelligent.

"Wait," Bakko said. "Something is—"

The fiend pounced across the bed, joints snapping. There was a blur of limbs as one of the its hands struck Bakko's pencil out of his paws and Kiri was knocked back by the other. A warped foot slammed into Bakko's chest. Unable to regain his balance, he tumbled over the edge of the bed. He barely grasped the padded comforter with a flailing paw. Kiri cried out above him.

"Hold on!" Bakko grunted.

He heaved himself up and rolled to his feet. Bakko scouted for the fiend, but it was gone. Kiri sat holding her head, her red ribbon discarded and dim.

Bakko panted. “Where did it go?”

She didn’t answer.

Bakko decided to worry about the fiend later. He jogged to Kiri and helped her to her feet.

“That fiend must have hit you hard,” Bakko said. “Did you see where it went? I can’t find it.”

Kiri shook her head, blinking. It passed too quickly for Bakko to be sure, but he could have sworn there was a glint of blue in Kiri’s good eye.

“All right,” Bakko picked up her ribbon and pressed it into her paw. “You can help me look for it once you’re ready.”

Bakko had only gone a few steps when he was aware of Kiri standing right behind him. She was close enough that the smell of old patchouli was nearly overwhelming. He was stopped dead in his tracks when Kiri's ribbon soared over his head and pulled tight around his throat.

Bakko pried madly at the ribbon, only to have Kiri tighten her pull. Incoherent thoughts uselessly piled on top of one another: Kiri shouldn’t be attacking him, he needed to do something, she had to let him go, something was very wrong.

He tried to gasp for air. The room grew hazy and black gathered at the edges of his vision. He sank to his knees as his legs gave out.

Desperate and losing consciousness, Bakko grabbed Kiri's paws and focused. It wasn’t easy, but before oblivion claimed his senses, magic flooded his core. He used his last ounce of concentration and forced his magic to his paws.

Kiri released the ribbon and drew back from the intense heat.

Ragged coughs racked Bakko's chest. Sucking in as much oxygen as he could, he lurched to his feet.

Kiri's face was inscrutable; a blank slate. Her head jerked, devoid of the grace that he knew her for. Everything came together for Bakko, all of the horrid pieces falling into place. The fiend had been hiding in plain sight.

Dropping to all fours, Kiri turned her attention from Bakko to the sleeping Girl behind him. She hauled herself across the bed on extremities that bowed and flipped out of sync with one another.

Bakko lunged. "No, Kiri!"

She wriggled and contorted in his grasp as he dragged her away from The Girl.

"Can you hear me?" Bakko pleaded. "Don't let it win!"

Kiri arched her back and thrust her knee into Bakko's stomach. The intense pang almost made him lose his grip. The fiend was wearing him down.

"Stop!"

She ignored him, wrestling to break free.

Bakko knew he was out of time to come up with a good plan. He didn't want to injure Kiri, but if he didn't do something soon, the fiend would use her to feed off of The Girl, and he couldn't let that happen.

"I'm sorry," Bakko whispered.

Using the extra weight he had over Kiri, Bakko wrapped his arms around her and pushed her down into the comforter. He closed his eyes and surged with magic. It didn't hurt him, but he could hear Kiri hiss sharply. She frantically struggled to wriggle out from his grasp. Bakko's eyes watered as a bitter taste filled his mouth.

Kiri went rigid, then limp in his embrace. Bakko let the magic fade and sat up, gingerly touching her shoulder.

Gray mist rose from her faded brown fur. Bakko instinctively recoiled. Beside her, the fiend reformed, unscathed by his magic burst. Keeping the fiend in view, Bakko felt for his pencil. Knowing that it could invade and control him made it even more frightening than before.

The fiend sprang. Bakko barely had time to react, raising his glowing pencil to fend it off.

One of its haunted blue eyes exploded when Bakko's pencil plunged in. A deluge of black ooze poured from the gaping hole framed with ragged bits of remaining tissue.

Paralyzed by the grisly image, Bakko didn't see the fiend's arm snap out until it was too late. His pencil went flying, the glow dying as it rolled underneath the dresser. Finger joints cracking, the fiend snatched Bakko's waist.

"Help! Kiri!" he wheezed.

She didn't move.

The fiend inched its mangled face closer. Clear liquid ran from the corners of the remaining eye, threatening to drip on him. Bakko attempted to recall the magic and blast his way out of the fiend's grasp, but he couldn't concentrate. Something about the eye was as mesmerizing as it was dreadful.

In the cocoon of the bedsheets, the sleeping Girl

sighed, breaking the eye's hypnotic effect just long enough for Bakko to come back to his senses.

With only a second to act, Bakko grabbed the fiend's eye, forcing both paws into the socket.

"Got you!"

Bakko allowed magic to fill him with more power than he'd ever experienced since Kiri had woken him. Squeezing the last watery eye, Bakko blasted with all of his might. The eye resisted him at first, but then it popped, spilling black slush all over Bakko's pink paws.

The fiend dropped Bakko, its head dipping and wrenching in voiceless pain. Black fluid continued to leak out of the empty sockets. It staggered back blindly until it misstepped and slipped off of the bed.

Breathing hard, he crawled to where the fiend had lost its footing. Bakko watched the fiend's convulsing death throes, its joints flailing and contracting. He couldn't help but smile as the fiend's crumpled frame melted, seeping between the floorboards.

It was over.

±Δ±

Kiri was propped against Bakko as he sat on the edge of the pillow. He watched her anxiously as the time between each of her breaths lengthened. She hadn't moved since he'd been forced to use his magic on her.

"I'm so sorry," he whispered.

The room began to brighten with morning light.

Bakko played the fight over and over again in his memory. He thought back to the moment where Kiri—Kiri with the fiend inside of her—had turned toward The Girl. There hadn't been time to think his actions through, only to do what he'd been trained to by Kiri. If there had been time, he might have done things differently.

More than anything, Bakko wished he could have just a minute more with Kiri. There were things that he still didn't know about being a Guardian which she could teach him. Most of all, he wanted to know if Kiri would have trusted him to take over the night watch.

The bedroom grew lighter.

Her body suddenly became warm, magic covering every inch of her.

"Kiri?"

The space around her filled with a glowing haze as the magic drifted away. Bakko's mouth hung open while he watched it dissipate into the bedroom air. When he looked back at her, everything was different. Her limbs lay rigid and her eyes stared blankly. He knew she was gone.

Bakko wanted to stay and finish saying goodbye, but he knew that he only had a minute until he fell asleep wherever he was. The last thing Kiri would have wanted was for him to arouse suspicion by falling asleep out of place where The Girl would notice.

As reverently as he could, Bakko laid the toy that had been Kiri the Guardian on the pillow. He climbed over the quilted comforter to the toy chest and pried the lid open. Before he lowered himself inside to sleep for the daytime, he glanced one more time at the stuffed bunny.

"I won't let you down." His voice broke.

Bakko dropped into the toy chest, closing the lid just as sunlight streamed into the bedroom.

Blinking against the rays that filtered through her curtains, The Girl pushed the covers off of her and let the cool morning air tingle across her skin.

She stopped, frowning. Lying on her pillow was the stuffed bunny that usually sat propped up on her headboard. The Girl scooped it up and studied its shabby brown fur and scratched eye. The old bunny was more tattered than she remembered. After some consideration, she tucked it under her arm and walked to the toy chest. Propping the lid open, she pulled out another stuffed animal, a pink bear gifted to her on her last birthday. Once she tucked the old bunny into the space where the bear had been, The Girl closed the toy chest.

She smiled as she fit the bear snugly between the headboard and the wall. If any of her toys could make her feel safe at night, this bear could.

HUNTING FOR MORE?

READ THESE GREAT TREASURE OF YEAR'S PAST BY THE UTAH HORROR WRITERS!

2019 Anthology

Some will resist. Others will give in willing. You may even find that you like the psychosis, of original Utah Horror. Thirty lunatics have come together to produce the finest and most original unpublished writings, since losing their minds. Experience the delusion and insanity of this new collection of horror in poetry, flash, and short fiction.

Hypnotic flesh eaters, ghosts of the past, ritual killings, time loops in hell, Ted Bundy's murder-sex, subdermal insects, homicidal hauntings, and asylum wanderers will thrill and fascinate you on the way out of sanity.

2018 Anthology

They say some only hunger for food, while others only hunger for love. But have they ever encountered a different kind of hunger: the insatiable, unstoppable appetite for fear?

Feast upon 24 never-before-published stories and poems fresh from the darkest minds in Utah's horror writing community. Sample the succulent flavors of dread and despair in these terrifying tales of ravenous zombies, piggish parasites, cannibalistic neighbors, and so much more.

When we crave the unnatural, there is no loyalty. There are no rules. There is only...THE HUNGER.

Not for the faint of heart, *The Hunger*: *A Collection of Utah Horror* is sure to satisfy your craving for something that will keep you up at night. Devour it...before it devours you.

2017 Anthology

Twelve Apocalyptic horsemen of the Rocky Mountains have come together in this terrifying anthology of Utah Horror. After years of dystopian fiction, these twelve writers won the challenge to portray how the apocalypse would occur.

Questionable kittens, ritualistic killing, destroying angels, ancient gods seeking punishment, lawless renegades, practitioners of the dark arts, and zombies will haunt every corner of your mind as you read these thrilling accounts of what could happen during the end of days in Utah.

Reanimated corpses of religious fanatics proclaiming salvation are the least of your worries...

2016 Anthology

The Great Salt Lake is a remnant of an ancient lake that was almost as long as the State of Utah. What mysteries does it hold in its briny waters? What secrets lurk in its murky shores?

...a malevolent spirit haunts a pregnant woman, luring her ever closer to the salty depths, yet what it wants is much more horrifying than death...the inversion and smog in the Salt Lake Valley carries more than just bad air...two locals find more than they bargain for when they unearth an ancient box buried in the salt-caked muck...

Whether its mystery, apparitions, ancient curses, or a modern day apocalypse, one thing holds all these tales together: The Great Salt Lake. Nestled inside the second anthology of Utah horror, are tales intended to delight a wide range of readers.

2015 Anthology

The West has always been a symbol of the wild frontier, rugged adventure, and dangerous exploration. However, if it wasn't for fear of the unknown, the West would just be another cardinal direction. *Old Scratch and Owl Hoots* delves into that fear and captures it in fourteen tales of terror set in the West ranging from the 1800s to the present day. Take a gander inside…a strange creature on Antelope Island that can never satisfy its hunger…a woman's vacation to Zion National Park that takes a dark turn when she can't stop hearing the cries of a newborn baby…an outlaw on the run from Porter Rockwell who finds more than he bargains for in the Utah wilderness…

Cozy up next to a campfire and delve into these fourteen stories and find out why it's dangerous to be out and about in the West when the sun goes down.

ARE YOU A HORROR WRITER?

The Utah Horror Writers formed in June, 2014. If you live in Northern Utah, consider joining the Chapter. The group is for new and old writers, published and unpublished. Find out more at www.utahhorror.org and on Facebook: Utah Horror Writers.

Call for Submissions

Each year the chapter publishes an anthology of local horror. A writer does not have to live in Utah, but the story must have a connection to Utah.

We are pleased to announce the 2021 anthology:

Wasatch Witches

Monsters, werewolves, vampires, and more, submissions will be accepted in four different categories:

-Flash Fiction: No greater than 1,000 words.

-Short Fiction: No greater than 5,000 words.

-Poetry: Up to 3 poems, no greater than 5 pages.

-Novelette: No greater than 15,000 words.

-Novella: No greater than 30,000 words

Accepted authors will receive payment per work. Multiple submissions welcome, but one per category. The call is open February 13 and closes October 31, 2020 at 11:59 pm, MST. Submit via email: utahhorror.anthology@gmail.com. Accepted authors will receive a small compensation.

Submit questions to utahhorrorwriters@gmail.com and see our website for submission guidelines.

www.ingramcontent.com/pod-product-compliance
Lightning Source LLC
Chambersburg PA
CBHW061922130726
47908CB00016B/997

* 9 7 8 1 7 3 4 0 0 6 7 6 6 *